Maury Had A Little Lamb

by
Janette Oke

Illustrated by
Brenda Mann

Other Janette Oke Children's Books in this Series—

SPUNKY'S DIARY
NEW KID IN TOWN
THE PRODIGAL CAT
DUCKTAILS
IMPATIENT TURTLE
A COTE OF MANY COLORS
PRAIRIE DOG TOWN

Copyright © 1989
by Bethel Publishing
Elkhart, IN 46516
All Rights Reserved
ISBN 0-934998-34-5

Printed in U.S.A.

Dedicated with our love to
Katherine Louise (Katie)
born December 18, 1988
to Lorne and Debbie Oke
and to
Courtney Elizabeth
baby sister for Ashley
born February 23, 1989
to Terry and Barbara Oke.

We, your grandparents,
and your cousins Nate and Jessica Logan,
welcome you to the family.

Table of Contents

Chapter One

Introductions

I blinked. The light was bright to my unaccustomed eyes. Somehow I knew that I had entered a new world. I wanted to look about me to discover all the newness but my eyes still wouldn't focus properly.

Strange squeals of excitement caused me to look up from where I rested on the soft bed of straw. I didn't know what had happened to cause all of the hubbub. It must be something pretty exciting.

Then something stirred near me. I turned my eyes toward whatever was moving and found that I was not alone. Beside me was an animal much bigger than I. I knew instinctively that this animal and I were very much a part of one another. I forgot the noisy shrieks and tried to lunge to my feet. I wanted to press myself as close as I could to the larger animal for protection.

My feet didn't work well at all. I was trying to discover just how to get them under myself. I heaved up with the front but the back legs didn't want to follow. I finally got the back ones in an upright position but the front ones went all haywire. Up and down, up and down I went; first front, then back, then

floundering in the straw again. I opened my mouth to call for help and the strangest little bleat came out. It surprised me. The objects leaning over the pen squealed even louder.

I knew that if I could gain my balance and get to the bigger animal, things would be just fine. I tried again— and finally I was able to stand on shaky, wobbly legs.

But just standing on my feet got me nowhere. What was I to do next?

Just then the big animal began to move. I studied her carefully. One foot, then the other foot. She was gliding across the pen toward me.

Then I noticed something else. I wasn't the only one of my size in the pen. Two other small animals tottered along beside the larger one. They were just like me. Well, almost like me. They were both larger than I was, even when I stood on my wobbly legs.

The big animal stopped moving and immediately the two smaller ones rushed to her side, butted up against her and began to enjoy some dinner.

It was then that I realized how hungry I was. I could smell the warm milk and it made me even hungrier. I pushed myself forward, one unsteady step at a time.

It took a few steps to catch on to how it was done. Once I landed back in the straw again, but I struggled to my feet and started toward the bigger animal.

I was almost there and feeling more and more excited when a strange thing happened. A terrible thing. She reached out with her nose and pushed me firmly away. The nudge upended me again and I went sprawling into the straw.

I bleated in protest. Hadn't she seen me coming? Didn't she know how hungry I was? I belonged to her too.

I decided that there must have been some mistake.

She couldn't really have meant to bump me. I struggled to my feet and tried again.

This time I was a bit more subtle. Instead of running directly for her head, I changed my course and headed for the other end. The other two were eating hungrily, slurping the warm milk noisily, the fluffy appendages on their back ends waving back and forth in appreciation. I could imagine just how good the dinner tasted.

I pushed my way forward and eagerly reached for the spigot. One of the nursing animals moved slightly to block my admittance.

"Hey," I complained. "I'm hungry too, you know. Can't you share?"

But he didn't even stop to answer me. The milk was dripping off his greedy chin.

I knew instinctively that I would get no dinner on his side, so I hastened around the big animal and tried the other feeder.

This animal did stop. For a moment.

"Can I try?" I asked.

He looked at me rather blankly.

"Can I have some?" I continued. "I'm awfully hungry. I haven't had anything to eat since—since—." I didn't know when I had eaten last. Truth was, I guess I had never eaten—but I sure wanted to eat now.

He stared hard at me. Then gave me a little butt.

"Get your own," he answered.

"But—but—this is my own," I trembled. "At least, I think it's my own. I mean—I'm here—this—this—."

I looked back at the larger animal.

"This—this is my mother, too. I think."

But the other animal wasn't listening. He went right back to his feeding, completely ignoring me and my need for dinner. I decided to push my way in. It didn't work. He was much bigger. He just moved so one of his shoulders blocked my way, and went right on nursing.

I gave up and went back to the other side again. At least the fellow there wasn't quite as big.

It didn't work there either. Try as I might, I made no headway at all. I decided it was time to appeal to the bigger animal. I headed to the front where I knew communications took place.

"They won't share," I began—but she just stared at me.

"I'm hungry," I persisted "They just eat and eat. They won't let me have my turn."

She sighed. Agitated. She seemed to feel that she was doing all she could; after all, she had worked hard enough for one day and wished to be left in peace.

"Please—," I begged her.

"Can't you see?" she said at last "There isn't room for more. I have two to care for already."

"But—," I began.

"There are lots of other sheep. One of the other ewes can care for you. I have all I can handle. Can't you see that?"

"But—."

It was really no use. She closed her eyes and I knew that she hoped I'd go away. I didn't. I just stood there, my tummy longing for some of the warm, sweet milk.

"Please," I said one more time.

She reached down and pushed me away. Rather roughly. I sprawled in the straw again. I didn't have the courage to try to get up. Suddenly warm hands were lifting me and the noises that I had heard began to change to individual voices.

"You poor little thing," someone was crooning. "Poor little thing. Your mama doesn't want triplets. She can't handle three. She's afraid if she tries to feed three, there won't be enough milk for everyone. Everyone will go hungry. You poor little thing."

The hands were consoling as they stroked back and forth over my curly, white coat. But the pain in my stomach didn't lessen.

"We'll find you another mama," said the voice, and then there was a loud screech that nearly scared me to death. "Da-ad."

I heard an answer from somewhere in the distance. "Yes-s."

"The ewe won't take her lamb."

"Which ewe?"

"Shanta."

I could hear footsteps approaching. "But I checked her just a few minutes ago. I thought she had accepted them both."

"But she has three—three."

"Are you sure?" The deeper voice had almost reached us now.

"I'm sure. See," and I was pushed toward a much bigger being.

He took me. His hands were much larger than the ones that had been holding me, but I felt a gentleness in them so that the fear I had felt soon left me.

"Well, I'll be!" he said as he moved forward to look in the pen. "Triplets."

He stood there quietly for a few minutes, chuckling to himself, his hand caressing the softness of my back.

"Well, Shanta," he went on, "you really did it this time. Nice looking pair you have there too." Then he looked down at me. "Now this one," he said, scratching my side, "This one isn't much. Tiniest little thing I ever saw."

The smaller person was beside us then and he was joined by another even smaller than himself. I knew as soon as I heard the voice that it was the smaller one

who had been doing the squealing.

"Isn't it cute, Daddy? Isn't it cute? It's so tiny. But the mama won't feed it. What will we do? It has to eat."

The bigger one cut in. "We'll find another ewe. One that has only one lamb—hey, Dad?"

"We can try," said the biggest. "But it doesn't always work. Sometimes they don't accept an orphan or outcast."

"He's hungry," insisted the smallest one. "I saw him. I saw him try and try to get some dinner but the other lambs and the mama wouldn't let him eat."

"He'll be hungry—that's for sure," agreed the biggest person.

"Let's hurry. Let's find a new mama."

We began our rounds then. I started out feeling excitement and a great deal of hunger. The excitement soon left me. But the hunger increased. Ewe after ewe turned her back on me, moved out of my reach or butted me away. It seemed that nobody wanted a skinny, brand-new, half-starved lamb.

"What'll we do Dad?" asked the now-familiar voice.

"I don't know, Maury. Guess there's only one thing to do. We'll have to bottle-feed him."

"Bottle-feed?"

There was more loud noise from the smallest one. "I will Daddy. I will. Can I? Can I please?"

The big one seemed to consider that for a moment, then he spoke again.

"Caring for a new-born lamb takes a great deal of time and attention. It's a big job, Jenny. Too big for you just yet. I think that Maury should take this one on—if he's interested. How about it Maury?"

I felt myself lifted eagerly from the larger hands to smaller ones. The boy named Maury cuddled me close, one hand under my chin so that he could look at my face.

"Sure," he said "Sure." I could hear the excitement in his voice.

"Come on then," said the father. "He's waited too long already. We'd better get some milk in that empty tummy."

It sure did sound good to me.

Chapter Two

Settling In

It seemed to take forever for them to get my bottle ready but finally they were pushing something toward me and I could smell warm milk. At first I was a bit awkward but I was so hungry that I persisted. At last it was working and I could feel the warm milk flowing down my throat and filling the big emptiness that I felt inside. Involuntarily my tail began to flick, back and forth, back and forth, in rhythmic motion. It felt so good to be getting something to eat.

After they were sure that I had enough, they began to talk again.

"Can I hold him? Can I hold him?" begged the one named Jenny.

"His tummy is full," warned Maury.

"I'll be careful. I'll hold still."

Another voice spoke. It was the one that the others called, "Mama."

"I think you'd better let him sleep now. He is just new-born you know—and very tiny. There'll be lots of time to hold him later. He needs to rest now if he is going to grow properly."

"Aw-w," Jenny whined.

"Tell you what," said Maury. "You can hold him while I fix him a bed. But you've got to hold him still. An' don't press on his tummy."

"I will. I won't," promised Jenny.

I was shifted from one pair of arms to the other. It jarred me a bit, even though they did try to be careful. I felt a strange, funny feeling and a bubble traveled all the way from my tummy to my mouth and made a soft little burp sound. Jenny laughed.

Then she settled me against her own small body and held me very carefully. Suddenly I felt so tired—so tired. I couldn't even hold my eyes open. I just wanted to curl right up and go to sleep. But I couldn't curl up the way Jenny was holding me.

"Now you remember," I heard the mama saying, "he's only to be in the house temporarily. He'll have to go out with the other sheep just as soon as he doesn't need to eat quite as often."

"I promise," agreed Maury.

"I'm not at all fond of the idea of a sheep in my house," she said with finality.

"I know," Maury conceded.

"And I don't want you coaxing to keep him here longer than is necessary."

"I won't," Maury promised.

I didn't know what all of the fuss was about. It was true that the house had some rather strange odors. It didn't smell nearly as nice as the warm, sweet straw—but I really didn't mind. I'd manage somehow.

I was lifted from Jenny's arms and placed into a nice cozy pen. The bottom was soft and snugly though it sure didn't smell like the straw. I was hoping that Maury would join me so that we could snuggle up together—but he didn't. I felt very lonely. I bleated—

and a hand reached in to stroke my woolly back. I felt a bit better then.

"Lie down," coaxed Maury. "Just lie down. You need to rest. You'll be warm here."

He gently eased me down on the softness. I was so tired I couldn't even protest. I curled myself into a ball, thankful for the freedom to do so. I tucked my chin against my body and let my eyes close. It felt so good just to relax. It felt so good to have a full tummy. It felt so good to have a hand stroking my back. I decided that I was going to like my new mother, Maury, and with that thought, I went to sleep.

I don't know how long I slept but when I awoke I was terribly hungry again. I scrambled to my feet and called out to Maury with a rather weak little "Baa-a."

He was right there—reaching for me, caressing my wool. Jenny was there, too.

"He's awake now—can I hold him?" she began.

"You can't always be holdin' him," protested Maury. "You'll spoil him."

"Just for a little while," argued Jenny.

"He's hungry again," stated Maury. "I need to get his bottle."

"Already? He just ate."

"Lambs eat often. 'Specially at first. An' he's little so he'll need to eat even oftener," explained Maury.

I bleated again. I wanted Maury to hurry and do something.

"He wants to be picked up," Jenny said.

"Well—okay. But only while I get his bottle ready," Maury agreed.

It wasn't long until Maury was back with my meal and fed me again. I was surprised after I finished the bottle that I felt tired. I didn't even complain much when Maury put me in my private box and told me to go back to sleep.

In fact, I spent the rest of the day that way—eating and sleeping by turn. Jenny would plead to hold me—Maury would agree to a few minutes while he prepared a bottle—and then I would be fed and bedded again.

At the end of the day my box was lifted and I was transported to another room.

"You're gonna sleep in here with me so I can hear you in the night," Maury explained.

He settled the box next to a large flat thing and then proceeded to change his whole covering. I didn't know that you could pull off one skin and pull on another in such a simple fashion. I looked down at my own woolly coat. It seemed secure enough. Maybe I was just too little yet.

Maury knelt beside his bed. I thought it was a very strange way to go to sleep. I knew that he would be much more comfortable if he curled up and tucked in his head. I wished that there was some way I could tell him so. But Maury was talking. I looked around to see if Jenny or the daddy or mama had come into the room but I saw nobody. It puzzled me. But maybe Maury had strange ways of communicating, I concluded. I knew that he sure had a strange way of shedding his coat.

Then as I listened I heard Maury say, "An' thank you for my new lamb. Help me to feed him and take care of him properly, just like Dad says. An' help me not to coax Mom when it is time to take him back to the sheep barn. Help him to grow fast and not to get sick or anything."

Maury went right on talking for a few minutes more and then he said, "Amen" and jumped back up again. I guess he didn't intend to sleep that way after all. I

began to feel excited. Perhaps he would join me in the box. Why else would he move the carton into his room? I moved over so Maury could climb in with me.

But Maury didn't climb in. Instead he went to the big, flat thing, tossed back the fluffy covers and snuggled deeply into the softness. It looked even softer than my bed. I decided that I'd prefer to sleep up there with Maury. I tried to tell him so—pushing myself as tightly as I could into the corner of the box toward the bed. I even tried to jump—but it was no use. My legs were still too wobbly for jumping. I bleated—and bleated again, but Maury didn't seem to understand what I was trying to tell him.

He rolled over and reached a hand down into the box, stroking me, talking quietly.

"It's time to go to sleep now, fella. Settle down. If you make so much noise Mom will really want you back in the barn. Sh-h, now. Sh-h. You'll keep everyone awake. We need to get some sleep. You'll wake up soon enough, wanting to be fed again. Sh-h now."

I decided that it was useless to argue. Maury just didn't understand what I was saying. At last I settled down in my own box and closed my eyes for sleep.

We were up several times in the night. Maury would yawn and mumble a bit but he didn't complain. Each time he tried to hush me and then he hurried off and was soon back with a bottle of warm milk.

As soon as I fed, I curled up and went to sleep again. Before I knew it, the darkness was gone and a warm, brightness filled our pen. Maury slept on. I couldn't understand why he needed so much sleep.

I was about to call him when the door opened and Jenny burst in.

"Maury—did the lamb wake you? Did he need to be fed in the night?"

Maury groaned and rolled over.

"Did you have to get up with him?" Jenny persisted, perching on the edge of Maury's bed.

"What do you think?" moaned Maury.

"Oh!" squealed Jenny. "He's awake now," and she reached down and scooped me up in her arms.

I liked Jenny. She seemed to be fond of me. But oh, my, she did let me dangle awkwardly as she tried to hold me. I squirmed.

"Now be nice," she scolded softly. "Don't try to get away."

"I s'pose he's hungry again," yawned Maury.

"Can I fix his bottle?" asked Jenny.

"Do you know how?"

"Mama will help me. She's getting breakfast."

"Okay—." Maury rolled over and shut his eyes again and Jenny flopped me down on the big bed beside him. Maury reached out one arm and drew me up against him. It felt good to be snuggled. The bed was soft just as I had known it would be. I couldn't understand why I hadn't been allowed to spend the night there. Perhaps Jenny understood. Maybe she was smarter than Maury. It didn't seem to take her long to figure out where I should be sleeping. I cuddled up against Maury and closed my eyes—but it was no use. I was too hungry to be able to sleep.

As soon as Jenny was back with the bottle, Maury rolled over again. He was still yawning but he lifted me onto his lap and gave me the nipple. I drank thirstily.

When the bottle was empty I expected Maury and I to settle back down in the soft bed again. It didn't happen that way.

"Mama says breakfast is ready," Jenny said and left the room. Maury climbed reluctantly from the covers, placed me back in my box and began to change his skin again. Then he spread up his covers, lifted my box and carried me back to the room where I had been before.

"Breakfast!" I heard the mama call.

"Comin'!" answered Maury. "I just need to wash."

I heard water running and then Maury's step as he headed for the pen they called the kitchen. They all began to talk together. I could hear Maury's voice, and Jenny's, then the mama and even the daddy but I was much too tired again to listen to the conversation.

I felt lonely without Maury. It had been so nice to snuggle up against him in his bed. Now that my tummy was full again I would really enjoy a sleep. I wished that he would come and get me and we could curl up together.

But Maury didn't come. At last I just gave up and curled up by myself. I needed the rest.

Chapter Three

Choosing A Name

"He needs a name." It was Jenny's voice that reached me. "We can't just call him Lamb all the time."

"I've been thinking about it," said Maury.

"I think we should call him Snowflake," continued Jenny.

"Naw."

"Why not? Look how white he is. 'Sides lambs are always called Snowflake."

But Maury wasn't convinced. "Not my lamb," he said.

"Snowball, then?"

"Snow nothin'," responded Maury. "They're dumb names."

"Well, then you pick a better one," challenged Jenny.

"I will," Maury informed her. "It won't be a 'Snow' somethin' either."

"Whitey?" ventured Jenny. "Curly? Downy?"

Each time, Maury shook his head.

"Cottontail?"

"That's for rabbits," snorted Maury.

"It could be for lambs, too, if you wanted it," Jenny argued, her lip sticking out and her chin lifting.

"Well, I don't want it. I don't even like it."

"You pick one then," Jenny prompted again.

"I will," Maury told her.

"Well—you sure are slow," Jenny chided.

"You just don't give me time—that's all. You don't name somebody the first thing you think of. You gotta choose a name carefully. Make it suit him."

Jenny stood to her feet and sighed a deep sigh. Then she turned on her heel and started from the room.

"He'll be an old, old sheep before you ever get him named," she called over her shoulder.

Maury did not seem ruffled at all. He set aside the bottle from which I had just had another meal and picked me up gently.

"You're a whole day old," he informed me. "I guess that's sorta your first birthday."

I didn't know what birthdays were but, from the way Maury spoke, I decided that they must be something good.

Maury ran a hand over my curly sides.

"You're still awfully little," he went on. "But you'll grow. By the way you're eating you'll grow in a hurry, Dad says."

I felt that 'to grow' must be good, too.

"Won't be long until you'll be sleepin' through the night, Dad says." Maury sounded wistful. I wondered what was so good about that.

"But you do need a name. I've tried an' tried to think of one and I just can't find one that suits you."

I agreed with Maury. I didn't care much for that Snowflake idea, though I had no idea what a snow-flake was.

"I know," called Jenny, bouncing back into the

room again. "Tiny."

But Maury just frowned and shook his head.

"Well, he is tiny," said Jenny defiantly, shaking her curls until they bounced.

"He won't always be tiny," Maury was quick to respond. "Dad says that the way he eats, he'll be big in no time."

Jenny left again.

I was getting sleepy but Maury went right on petting me, stroking my sides and talking.

"Your mom's name is Shanta. Mom called her that. She names almost all of our sheep. Shanta. I like that name. It suits. But I've tried and tried to think of a name that suits you and I just can't."

Maury put me back to bed and left the room. I didn't sleep very long. When I woke up it wasn't because I was hungry. I was just tired of being tired, I guess. My legs felt funny. Like they needed to stretch—or jump— or something.

Maury must have heard me stirring about. He came into the room.

"What's the matter, Lamb?" he asked me, bending to scratch my ear. "You can't be hungry already."

The mama lady came to stand beside Maury. She looked down at the box-bed.

"Maybe he needs some exercise," she suggested. "It's a nice day. Why don't you take him out and let him run around the yard for a while?"

Maury lifted me and started from the room. As he walked toward the door he grabbed a light jacket from a hook and wiggled his way into it, one arm at a time.

"It's a little cold," he informed me. "Just a little. It's still early spring, you know."

I didn't know—but I was quite willing to accept Maury's word for it.

When we got to the yard Maury set me down. He was right. It felt cold. Patches of white stuff lay against the fence and stacked up even higher in one corner. Beneath me, dried straw-stuff seemed to be growing right out of the ground. I sniffed at it but I didn't really like the smell. I looked back up at Maury.

"Come on," he coaxed. "Run around a little."

He started to move away from me and I panicked at the thought of being alone. "Baa-a," I cried and ran after him.

Maury began to laugh. I guess he thought that I sounded funny.

"C'mon," he called. "Run faster."

I was surprised at how much better my legs were working. Why, yesterday I could barely stand and here I was chasing after Maury.

Maury was laughing now. "C'mon," he called again. "C'mon."

I followed after him, round and round the pen called the yard. I soon realized that we were playing some kind of game. I liked it. My legs liked it. It made them feel much better to stretch a bit. I even tried a couple jumps just to see if they would work. They did. I jumped again, twisting sideways in the air before I lit. Maury laughed.

"You're pretty frisky," he called, "maybe that's what I should call you. Frisky."

Maury seemed to consider the name for a minute. "Naw," he said at last, "We already have a Frisky. Can't name you that."

I ran and jumped and chased Maury until my legs began to tire. Then I decided to slow down a bit and check out the yard-pen. Maury was still running around but I let him play by himself.

I was plenty warm enough now. The running

seemed to have done that for me. I no longer felt restless, just curious. I crossed to where the white stuff lay and stuck my nose in it just to see what it smelled like. It was cold—and it didn't smell good either. In fact, it didn't have much smell at all. I sneezed and snorted, shaking the coldness from me. It was silly stuff, this white. I left it and went to check out other things.

Near the house was a long, long coiled green thing. I sniffed at it but it was cold and lifeless and didn't appear to be good for anything. I let it hang where it was. Next I ran to the side of the yard-pen and sniffed at some funny looking straw-things that poked up above the white stuff. Some of it smelled good—some didn't smell good at all. I wondered what it was but just then Maury called, "Hey, you'd better stay out of Mom's flower beds. She'll be mad if you pull up the flowers before they get a chance to grow."

I knew by the tone of Maury's voice that I'd better get out of there.

I was just going to check out a funny little house that stood in a corner when the strangest thing happened. A great big animal poked out a nose and then came right toward me. I stopped dead in my tracks, my mind saying that I should run for Maury but my legs refusing to take a step. The big thing came nearer and nearer. I just stood there shaking, shivering in fear. I was sure that it was going to eat me up right where I stood.

"Baa-a," I called, wanting Maury to come quickly and save me.

The big thing reached out a long nose. Then he took a lick. I was sure that he was just sampling, to see if he really wanted to eat me or not. I could see many sharp teeth in his mouth as he ran his tongue over his lips.

"Baa-a," I said again.

And then, as if by some miracle, Maury was at my side. But he didn't scoop me up quickly and run as I had hoped he would. Instead he plopped himself down on the ground beside me.

"I've got a new lamb, Buster," he said, reaching out a hand to stroke the big animal. "Isn't he cute? You can help me look after him. His mother had triplets and couldn't take care of 'em all so I get to raise him."

I guess the big animal, Buster, wasn't too impressed. At any rate he turned his back on both of us and walked slowly back to his house in the corner. I was greatly relieved.

"That's Buster," Maury told me. "He's our sheep dog. He's really good with sheep. We have two dogs. Buster and Babs."

Maury did pick me up then. I was still shivering.

"Hey, you're cold," said Maury. "I'd better get you in."

There was no way that I could tell Maury that I'd just been scared half out of my wits.

"Mom," said Maury that evening. "Would you help me?"

His mother looked up from the book she was holding.

"I need a name for my lamb."

"He's so fussy," cut in Jenny. "I said lots of names—an' he didn't like any of them."

"What kind of name are you thinking of?" the mother asked.

"Well—I don't want anything with Snow. An' I don't want Tiny or Peewee or anything like that," Maury informed her.

She seemed to think about that.

"I sorta like Frisky," went on Maury, "but we've

already got a Frisky."

"You could call him Skippy," said Jenny. "We don't got a Skippy."

But Maury just frowned and shook his head.

"I want something that suits him," he told his mother.

"And you think Frisky suits him?" she said.

"Yeah. It does. But we've used it already. I like his mother's name, Shanta. But we can't call him Shanta, too."

"Maybe we can find a name something like Shanta. Run and get the name book. It's on the fireplace bookshelf."

Maury ran and was soon back with a book in his hand. He climbed up beside his mother while she flipped through the book. Jenny crawled up on the other side.

"Sean. Seldon. Seth. Seymour," she read, but with each name Maury shook his head.

"Shalom. Shamus. Shandy. Oh, look at this. Shandy means 'rambunctious'."

"What's rambunctious?" asked Maury.

"That's almost like frisky," said his mother.

"It is?" Maury's eyes were big. He was thinking about the name.

"It sounds almost like Shanta," said Jenny.

"And it really means frisky?" asked Maury.

"That's what the book says," his mother nodded.

"Shandy," said Maury. "Shandy. I kinda like it. It's different. And it suits him." He began to grin. "Yeah, I think I'll call him Shandy. Thanks Mom."

"You're welcome," said his mother, closing the book and passing it to Maury. "And now it's bedtime. I would suggest that you give your Shandy one last bottle and then get ready for bed."

Maury scooped me up, pen-box and all, and moved me off to the kitchen.

"Shandy," he said. I didn't know if he was talking to me or himself. "Shandy. I like it. Do you like it? I think it suits you."

"Baa-a," I said in reply. I really didn't care that much what Maury decided to call me. What I was interested in was the bottle his mother had spoken of. For some reason I was hungry—again.

Chapter Four

Changes

A few mornings later a strange, sad thing happened. Maury and Jenny both seemed to be rushing madly about the house. Maury had given me my breakfast but I sensed that something was different about the way he held me—about the way he urged me to finish the bottle quickly.

As soon as I had swallowed the last drop he deposited me back in my box and almost ran from the room. I could hear the family in the kitchen.

"Well," said the father, "your little break is over. It's back to school again for you."

Jenny seemed excited about it. She talked non-stop. Finally the mother asked her to finish her breakfast so she wouldn't be late for the school bus. Jenny stopped talking—at least for a minute.

"What you gonna do 'bout Shandy?" Jenny asked around a mouthful of something.

"Mom's gonna feed him," came the reply from Maury.

"Bet he'll be lonesome," continued Jenny.

"I'll only be gone about six and a half hours," answered Maury. I didn't understand anything about hours but Maury seemed to feel that it wouldn't be too long until he'd be home again.

"He'll still be lonesome."

"I can't help it," said Maury. "I have to go to school." Then there was a pause. "Don't I?" asked Maury with pleading in his voice.

"You certainly do," replied his mother. "Don't worry. I've fed many a lamb in my day. Shandy and I will get along just fine."

"I—I wasn't really worried about his bottle," said Maury. "I—I was just thinkin' that he might miss me."

"Oh, he will—but he'll be fine," his mother promised. "Now you'd better hurry or you'll miss the bus."

I really wasn't too worried. All of the family had been gone for a time the day before. At first it had frightened me even though Maury had come, all dressed up in fine-looking new skins, his face shining and his hair slicked back, and told me not to worry, he'd soon be home again.

I had worried. At first. It was quiet and lonely in the house. I longed for company. I longed to hear someone stirring about. I had just been fed so I wasn't hungry—and then I fell fast asleep and didn't waken until I heard the door open and Maury was bursting into the room with Jenny close behind him. They were back. And it really hadn't seemed long at all—just as Maury had said.

But this—school—. I didn't know what to think of it. Maury's voice sounded worried. Not as it had sounded the day before.

Soon Maury was kneeling beside my box. His hand ran over my back and then stroked my head.

"Sorry, Shandy," he said and his voice sounded sad.

"Sorry. Our break is over. I have to go back to school today."

Jenny came to peek in at me, too. Maury was still stroking me.

"Mom will take care of you," Maury went on. "She'll give you your bottle. An' I'll be home just as soon as I can."

Maury was gone then and I was alone in the room—alone in my box-pen. I heard the door slam and then the house was quiet. I thought that I was all alone until I heard stirring in the kitchen. The mother was still with me. I called to her—but she didn't answer. I called again.

The door opened and she came into the room.

"What's the matter with you?" she asked me. "You've just been fed."

I wanted out. I wanted to be held. I wanted to follow her back to the kitchen.

"Baa-a," I said again.

"I have work to do," she told me. "You just settle down there and have a nap."

I didn't feel tired.

"Go on now. I haven't time to be spoiling a lamb."

She left me then and went back to her kitchen. I heard her as she moved about, doing different tasks.

At last I gave up. I curled into a ball and tried to sleep.

It was a long time before I was able to drop off. And then I didn't sleep for long. I stood to my feet and started calling again. I tried to jump up so that I could hook my front feet and tumble myself free of the box. The house was awfully quiet. I was afraid that there was no one home.

I was still too small to reach the top of the box—even when I jumped as high as my legs would take me. I

had been growing. I knew I had. And Maury was always telling me how quickly I was filling out. Even his father talked about it. Still—I hadn't grown enough yet. The box-pen still held me prisoner.

"Baa-a," I called as loudly as I could.

She came in then, wiping her hands on her apron. In her hands she held my bottle.

"So you want to eat again? Well, here you are." She knelt down beside the box.

"Here you go," she continued.

She didn't lift me from the box and hold me as Maury always did. Instead she held the bottle out to me and laughed as I took the nipple in my mouth.

"My, you are hungry. No wonder you are growing so quickly. Just look at you."

I gave a little bunt with my head and began to drink even faster. My tail whipped back and forth, back and forth. The milk began to drip from a corner of my mouth. The mother started to laugh.

"Hey, slow down," she chuckled. "You don't need to be in such a hurry. I'm not going to take it away until you're all finished."

True to her word, she waited right there until I had completely drained the bottle. I thought that she would pick me up and hold me then, but she didn't.

"There you go," she said and stroked my back "You should feel just fine, now."

I didn't feel fine. I just felt full. I still felt lonesome. I tried to tell her so.

"Now lie back down and have another nap," she told me. "Before you know it Maury will be home and then he'll take you for a little run."

But the day seemed to drag on and on and Maury didn't come. I couldn't sleep. I was much too lonesome. I would be so relieved when the long, long day of school was finally over and things would return to normal again. I was fed again—but I wasn't held that time either. I wanted Maury. Would he never return? I would even have settled for Jenny.

I had decided that something terrible had happened and Maury wouldn't be coming back when I heard the door bang. Maury hurried into the room, scattering lunchpail, books and his jacket behind him.

"Shandy," he called. "Shandy—I'm home."

Oh, I was glad to see him. He scooped me up and held me close, stroking my sides and telling me how much he had missed me. I wanted to tell him that I had missed him, too, but I didn't know how to say it. I was so glad that the long day was finally over.

I was shocked and saddened the next morning when Maury announced that he was off to school again. I couldn't bear the thought of another long day without him—even if he did hold me and play with me when he finally got home in the afternoon. But somehow, I made it through that day also.

Day followed day. I gradually adjusted to being alone. Then, just when I thought that I had finally sorted it out, another strange thing happened. Maury was home again. Oh, I was glad to have it all finished. It was so nice to have company for the whole day. We ran and played together in the big yard-pen. It felt good to get so much exercise. I was beginning to feel cramped and crowded in my box-pen.

The next day Maury came in all dressed up again. "We won't be gone long," he told me. "We'll be home right after church."

At first, I felt rather panicky, but I soon settled down and sure enough—I was still sleeping when they all returned.

But the next morning—it happened again. Maury

and Jenny rushed all around and then they were off to school again. I was heartbroken. I thought we were all through with that. But morning after morning it was the same. Hurry, hurry, hurry and then off to the school bus while I pined and complained all alone in my box-pen.

I was fed regularly—and I wasn't cold. My box was always clean. I had nice, soft bedding. But I was lonesome and unhappy until I heard the slam of the door and knew that Maury was home.

"Maury, I think it's time for Shandy to be moved out of the house." It was the mother's voice speaking.

"Aw," began Maury, but he was quickly stopped.

"Remember! No coaxing. You promised. The days are much warmer now. Look at him. He's getting too big for that box. He'll soon be jumping out. He almost did yesterday."

So she had noticed. I thought she wasn't looking. I had almost made it and I was sure that soon the box wouldn't hold me captive anymore. I would be free to come and go—just like the other people.

"But—," began Maury.

"No buts. He's perfectly big enough to be out in the barn with the other sheep. He doesn't need to eat nearly as often anymore."

"All right," Maury conceded reluctantly.

Maury picked me up and carried me outside. Together we headed for the big barn across the yard.

"You're gonna live with the other sheep," he told me. "You won't be lonesome there."

We entered the barn and Maury leaned over a wooden enclosure and set me gently on the floor. I recognized the smell. It was the nice smelling straw again.

"There you go," he prompted me. "Go make some friends." He nudged me forward gently.

I hesitated. I wasn't sure what I should do. I did see several lambs about my size and thought it might be fun to get to know them.

Just as I was about to move forward, a big ewe came toward me. Close at her heels was another ewe of the flock. They came a step or two at a time. Then a pause, then a forward movement again. At last they were close enough to reach out and sniff at my coat.

I stood stock still, shivering with excitement. I was just ready to bound forward excitedly when the first ewe snorted and exclaimed, "What are you doing here? You're a stranger. I don't even know you. You don't belong in this pen."

"What?" said the other. "A stranger? How'd he get in here? Where are the dogs?"

I made the mistake of moving then. Just one little tentative step forward—but it was one too many. The first ewe caught me solidly with the top of her head. The blow made me stagger. I was just finding my feet when the other ewe gave me another butt. I cried out, afraid for my life.

Then I felt hands lifting me. Maury was there. He had rescued me just in time.

"They don't want you," he said as he stroked me gently. "They don't even want you. They think that you might hurt their lambs. Silly old sheep. You can't go in there. I'll tell Mom."

And talking and stroking, he took me back to the house.

Chapter Five

A New Home

"The sheep don't like Shandy," Maury informed his mother.

"What do you mean, they don't like him?"

"They don't. They butted him. They even ganged up on him. Honest."

The mother stood looking down at me as I lay in Maury's arms. I was hoping she would decide that I could live right here. Oh, not in the box-pen. She was right about that. I had grown out of it. But there was plenty of room to run and play in the big house. I would be quite happy to live there with Maury and Jenny and the family.

"Well, he can't stay in here," the mother was saying. "I guess you'll have to build him a pen of his own.

"But—."

"Tomorrow is Saturday. Your father will help you. You can fix him his own pen in the sheep barn."

"Can he—can he stay in here—tonight?"

"Just for tonight. No more."

It seemed to be settled. But I was glad for the promise of one more night.

That night when Maury gave me my last bottle and settled down for bed, he reached down to rub my sides as he always did.

"This is the last night you can sleep in here, you know," he told me. "From now on you'll be sleeping out in the barn with the other sheep. I won't be able to bring you back in the house—cause you won't be as clean—won't smell the same. Mom will never let you in the house then."

The thought seemed to sadden Maury. His hand lingered on my head.

"They didn't like you," he went on. "You haven't done one thing to hurt them. But sheep are kinda dumb sometimes. They didn't even know that you are one of them. They thought that you might hurt their babies. Sheep don't go by looks. They go by smell—an' livin' in here with us all the time—well, you don't smell much like a sheep, I guess."

Maury stopped and thought about this for a moment. Then he spoke again.

"You know, even if you had smelled like a sheep, they might not have wanted you. 'Cause they didn't know you. Sometimes they don't even want other sheep in their pens. Not 'til they get to know them by their smell. Once they get used to them, they're okay, but I saw them chase two new sheep that Dad put in the pen once. But they were big sheep. They could take care of themselves. An' soon the flock got used to them and didn't bother them anymore. But you—you're too little to take care of yourself.

Maury's hand still kept stroking me.

"You've grown a lot," he said, "but you're still pretty little."

The thought seemed to sadden him. Before I knew it I was being scooped up out of my box-pen and snuggled down in his soft bed beside him.

"Now you be good," Maury cautioned. "Mom won't forgive you—or me—if you're not. An' this is the last time you'll ever have a chance to sleep with me—so you be good."

We curled up together. I'm not sure which one of us fell asleep first but when I opened my eyes again the sun was gently beaming in our window. Maury stirred just as I did. He hastily picked me up and put me gently into my box. Then he checked his bed carefully, throwing back the covers to be sure everything looked clean and tidy. He smiled.

"Mom will never know you slept with me," he said, then sobered. "Unless she asks. If she asks, I'll have to tell her the truth."

I was hungry. I wasn't worried about Maury's bed. I wanted my breakfast.

"I'm goin', I'm goin'." said Maury. And he headed for the kitchen and the bottle of milk.

During breakfast Maury and his father discussed my pen.

"Are you sure he wouldn't be happier in with the other lambs?" asked the dad.

"He might—enjoy the lambs, that is—but the ewes don't want him. They butt him and nearly knock him down," explained Maury.

"I suppose he might make them a bit upset. They aren't used to him."

"I think he should be alone—so he's safe," Maury continued.

"I guess we have room to give one wee lamb a home

of his own," answered the father.

After breakfast Maury picked me up and we all went to the big sheep barn. Even Jenny donned her jacket and joined us.

It was a beautiful spring morning and the smell of the fresh air and the sun warming the ground made me wish that I could get down and run.

"I think that I'll be able to let the sheep out to pasture soon," Maury's father was saying. He looked at the sky and smiled at the day.

"Bet Shandy would love to run around the pasture," Maury replied. Without really knowing anything about the pasture, I quite agreed with him. I was ready to run almost anywhere.

We reached the barn and Maury deposited me on the floor. I was able to run back and forth between the pens without fear of a large ewe giving me a good solid butt.

I did cause some commotion though. Ewes pressed against their enclosures, sniffing and snorting and warning me to keep my distance. Lambs pushed against the fences, too, but they didn't seem to care. I was sure that we could have had a good time playing together if we'd been given the chance.

The hammers began to pound and right before my eyes I saw a small pen taking shape. The father seemed quite pleased with it—but Maury looked doubtful.

"There," said the man "that's nice and strong—and just the right size, too. Big enough for him to stretch his legs, but not so big that he will feel forsaken."

Maury studied the pen.

"Are you sure that he—that he won't feel awfully lonesome?" he asked at last.

"Lonesome? Oh, maybe a little. At first. Remember, he's had an awful lot of attention for a little fella. I suppose he'll miss all the fussing for awhile. But he has the other sheep here. Even if he isn't in the same pens with them, he still will know that he's not alone. He can hear them, and smell them. He can even look through the boards and see them."

Maury didn't look too convinced.

"Now why don't you get him all settled in?" suggested the father. "I have other work to do."

Maury picked me up and started for the door.

"Where ya goin'?" yelled Jenny, who had busied herself with hand-feeding some of the ewes in one of the other pens.

"To the house," said Maury.

"I thought Mom and Dad said that Shandy was to live here."

"He is. I'm just going to get his box."

"He doesn't need his box now. He's got a pen."

"I know. But I thought that he might get lonesome for it. He's used to sleeping in it."

"Oh," said Jenny, and nodded in understanding. She stuffed another handful of hay between the rails to a large ewe who was munching contentedly. "Do you want me to run and get it?" she asked.

"Would you?"

"Sure. If you want me to."

Maury let a hand slide across my back. "That would be good," he said. "I'll stay here with Shandy in his new pen and get him used to it."

Maury placed me in the pen and then climbed in with me. He reached out a hand to me but he didn't pick me up.

"This is your new home Shandy," he informed me. "See, it's big enough for you to run—but not too big. Here. See, it has straw on the floor—just like the other sheep. You'll like it here."

Across from us the sheep were talking but I didn't even try to listen in on the conversation. Some lambs were playing a little game of leapfrog. From where I stood I could follow the game through the spaces between the boards. It looked like fun. I would have loved to join them. Then I thought of the big ewes with their hard heads and their cross looks and quickly changed my mind.

I listened then. Two ewes stood apart. They were still fussing and complaining that I had been brought right into their barn. Two others argued in the corner over who had the right to the last handful of hay that Jenny had thrown into the pen.

Back against the far wall three ewes lay close together, serenely chewing their cuds and visiting with one another. Here and there lambs frolicked or slept as the mood moved them. It was interesting to watch the pen of sheep. Beyond their pen, I could see other pens. They seemed to stretch on and on. I wondered briefly why they didn't all live together, but before I could try to sort it out, Jenny was back with my sleeping box.

"How's he gonna get in and out?" she asked as she came struggling in, puffing with the effort of carrying the box so far.

"I'll tip it on its side," answered Maury.

"Are you gonna leave the soft blanket? He's got hay now."

"Does Mom want it back?"

"She didn't say. I guess not. It's a ragged one anyway. She'd prob'ly just give it to Babs when she has her puppies," Jenny panted as she leaned against the pen and tried to catch her breath.

"Shandy needs it just as much as Babs does," decided Maury. "He knows it already. He knows its smell. He won't feel as lonesome with it here to sleep on. After he gets used to the straw we can take it out if we want to and wash it up for Babs."

Jenny seemed to agree. She said nothing more, just watched as Maury upended the box on its side and settled the blanket for my bed.

"There. There you are. Now you curl right up here and go to sleep. I'll be back soon with your bottle. I need to do my other chores now. Here. Lie down. You won't be lonesome. You have all the other sheep."

Maury pushed me into my box and tried to get me to lie down. I resisted—my legs stiff so they wouldn't bend. He gave up.

"Well, stand up then if you want to—but when you get tired, go to bed in here. I'll be back soon."

And with those words Maury and Jenny left me.

It was strange being in the barn without them. It was even stranger being with all the sheep—though I really wasn't with any of them. Still I could see them. Could hear them. Could smell them. I was very aware that they were right there in the same barn where I was.

And I knew that they were very aware of me also. I could still hear them talking. I could see them casting nervous or disdainful glances my way. Occasionally one sniffed or snorted and tossed her head.

The lambs seemed to pay little attention to me. I could have been invisible for all the recognition I got. They were much too busy with their nursing, their napping and their play to pay any attention to me.

I watched until I tired of it and then I went back to my familiar box and blanket and curled up for a nap.

Chapter Six

Adjustments

Each day when Maury returned from school he would come to the sheep barn and we'd spend some time playing together in the yard. The piles of white stuff had now disappeared and in their place, green began to show.

I liked the green much better. I soon discovered that it tasted even better than it looked. Maury said it was called grass. It was juicy and sweet and I couldn't seem to get enough of it. I wanted to share it with Maury but he didn't seem one bit interested in trying it.

I still had my bottle. I would have been lost without it, but the green grass tasted good, too.

Day by day, other green began to make an appearance. I was sure that it would taste just as good as the grass but everytime I headed for it, I was shooed away by Maury.

"Stay out of Mom's flower beds," he'd scold, "or she'll have your hide."

I went back to eating the grass again—but I did sorta keep my eye open just in case Maury got busy with something else.

It wasn't too bad living in the sheep barn. Oh, it was still lonesome being shut up all by myself. The sheep seemed to get used to my being there, but they never did extend a welcome.

Occasionally a lamb would look my way but its mother would nudge it aside and warn it about speaking to strangers.

The sheep dogs came and went as they wished. The ewes would lift their heads and sniff the air and shuffle about but eventually they would quiet down again and begin to feed.

The dog they called Babs spent more and more time in the barn. I wondered why. The weather was beautiful outside. I would have preferred to be out if I could have gone in and out at my own choice.

But there she lay, head on her paws, fat and docile and not very energetic.

One day the entire barn was in an uproar. I could hear them all talking before I even lifted my head from my blanket.

"Are you sure?" one ewe was asking another. "I didn't hear anything about it."

"Well, you weren't listening then," the first one snapped back. "I heard him say, right out. Today, he said. I heard it myself."

"Hmm-mm," sniffed a third. "I'll believe it when I see it."

The first ewe turned aside. I could see she was miffed. She said nothing more, just went to a corner and roused her lamb. The baby looked surprised at the nudging but scrambled to her feet with a little bleat and then went right to work nursing. The ewe was still looking down her nose at the other two.

"What was that all about?" asked a fourth one.

"She," said the second ewe, tossing her head toward the one standing in the corner, "she says that she heard him say that he is turning us out on the pasture grass today."

The fourth ewe sort of smiled. "Pasture grass. Oh, boy! It seems just years since I've had pasture grass."

"Well," sniffed number three. "I still say, I'll believe it when I see it," and she flung a look in the direction of the pouting ewe again.

Another ewe moved up to join the others. "Well, it's time, I'd say. Seems to me that we should have been out there a week ago."

She sniffed in impatience and stamped a foot.

Babies began to awaken then. They all seemed to be hungry at once and they started to run hither and yon through the cluster of ewes, sorting out which one was their mother. Soon they were all nursing, their tails jerking back and forth as they fed.

The lambs had not finished their breakfast when the man appeared. The sheep pushed forward, pressing against the wooden bars of the enclosure. What a commotion they made, asking him if today was really the day.

He ignored their questioning and came directly to me. "Here's your morning bottle Shandy," he said. "Maury was a little late this morning and had to leave for school." He held the bottle out to me and I drank eagerly. The sight of the lambs all having their breakfast had made me hungry. Soon I was licking at the last few drops. The man pulled the bottle from me.

"That's all," he laughed. "You've emptied it already. Boy, what an appetite. I don't think you ever get filled up."

He rubbed my back for a moment and then straightened.

"Well, Shandy. You might feel rather lonesome for the next few days. I'm turning the rest out to pasture today."

None of the others seemed to have heard. They still bleated and tramped about, trying to learn what the man intended to do.

"Of course they'll all be back in at night for awhile. That will give you company for sleeping." He rubbed my ear again.

So the ewe had been right. Today was the day.

The man went to one end of the barn and opened a low door. Then he whistled and Buster came bounding into the barn. Babs responded, too, but not too eagerly.

"It's alright, girl," the man said, reaching out to scratch her ear. "We won't need you today. Go lie down."

The dog went back to her soft hay, seemingly glad to be excused.

All of the sheep were on their feet already. Lambs were brushed aside whether they were finished with their breakfast or not. Ewes pressed forward, their noses to the boards of the pens. What a racket. It seemed each one was begging to be the first one out.

The ewe that had been pouting in the corner lifted her head and gave the others a scornful look. I couldn't hear what she said because of the din but I was sure that she must have said that she'd told them so. Maybe next time they wouldn't question her word.

Down the row of pens the man and dog worked slowly, as he opened one gate after another. Each time a gate was opened the ewes bolted forward, lambs at their heels. The dog stood quietly aside, making sure the sheep moved through the doorway instead of scattering around the barn.

But no one argued. None of the sheep had any desire to stay in the confines of the barn. As one, they darted toward the open gate anxious to reach the pasture and green grass they had been looking forward to. The poor lambs nearly got trampled in the rush, but somehow they managed to stay upright and out from under the rushing feet.

At last all of the gates had been opened and a strange quiet settled over the barn. The man picked up my empty bottle and started for the door. Buster walked quietly behind him. Soon the door closed and they were gone.

I looked over at Babs. Her ears were still alert but she looked agitated and tired.

"Finally," she said. "Finally, some peace and quiet."

She laid her head back down on her paws and closed her eyes. I watched her for a moment and then pressed against the wooden rail. It was so quiet. So—so lifeless. There was nothing to see and even less to do. I didn't have room to run and skip. There wasn't a soul stirring about. There were no conversations to listen to. No lambs to watch as they frolicked about. Boy! What a boring day this was going to be.

I looked again toward Babs. She was still lying there, head on her paws. And then a strange thing happened. She stood to her feet and moved about restlessly. She paced a few steps and then lay back down. She stirred herself again as though agitated and returned to her straw bed.

I figured that she must be as bored as I was.

"Wanna play some tag?" I asked her.

She gave me a withering look and put her head back down.

"Leapfrog?" I asked.

Babs didn't even answer me, just stood up, shook

herself slightly and moved all the way down the barn. She crossed into the far pen and I didn't see her again for the rest of the day.

"Boy," I said to myself. "What a poor sport. A lot of fun she turns out to be."

I settled myself into waiting for the school bus to bring Maury home. It was going to be another long, long day. I would be so glad to see him again. So glad to have a chance to run about the yard playing tag or hide and seek. So glad to be able to really stretch my legs.

I curled up in a corner and tried to go back to sleep. I didn't even bother with my blanket but lay right down on the straw. I was lonely and feeling sorry for myself. It didn't seem fair. Not fair at all. Here I was, the only one to be stuck inside the barn. It was a nice day, too. I could smell the fresh air and feel the warmth of the sunshine coming through the open door at the end of the barn. I wanted to cry—but there was no one to hear me so I just curled up tightly and tried to shut out everything. And I hoped with all of my heart that Maury would hurry home.

Chapter Seven

New Arrivals

The day seemed to drag on and on. I tried to sleep, got up and paced my little pen, tried to sleep again, took a few jumps and skips, tried to sleep again, but mostly just waited—and waited.

I didn't know where Babs had gone but I didn't see her again. I kept thinking of all the sheep enjoying the meadow grass, the sun and the spring freshness. For a moment I wished that I was a sheep—instead of a member of Maury's family. But I quickly put that thought aside. I loved Maury.

I was ready to give up when the barn door opened. I pressed myself against the wooden enclosure and called out to Maury, saying how glad I was to see him.

But it wasn't Maury. It was Jenny who came bouncing in.

"Hi, Shandy," she called as she came. "Maury went to get your bottle. Are you hungry?"

It was a silly question. I was always hungry.

"Boy, it's quiet in here with all of the other sheep gone," Jenny went on.

It certainly wasn't news to me.

Then Jenny left me without so much as a pat and went exploring throughout the big sheep barn. I called after her, but she just ignored my pleas.

"Maury will soon be here," she flung over her shoulder and went climbing from one sheep pen to another.

I heard her squeal at the same time that Maury came in the door. His appearance made her squeal again.

"Maury," she shouted. "Maury—come quick. Babs has her puppies."

"What?"

"Babs—she has her puppies. Down here. In this last pen."

So that was where Babs was. But what were puppies?

It must be something pretty important because Maury didn't even wait to say hello to me. He placed the full bottle on a post and darted off in the direction of Jenny.

"There're seven of them," Jenny was calling. "Seven—and they are so cute."

I watched Maury climb over the wooden barrier and then both he and Jenny seemed to be in a state of delirium. They called and squealed and shouted all at once. They sounded awfully excited—and happy.

"Look at this one—look at this one," Jenny kept insisting and then Maury would respond with some comment about how big it was or how small it was or how it was colored. This went on and on. I was beginning to wonder if they'd forgotten all about me. My eyes went back to the bottle forgotten on the post. I cried. I called to Maury. But no one heard me.

"Mama will want to see them," Jenny exclaimed.

"Run and get her," replied Maury.

"You run. You can run faster."

"You just don't want to leave the puppies," accused Maury.

"Well—," said Jenny, "you don't either."

I guess Maury agreed to that, but he didn't confess it. Instead he thought of something else.

"I still have to feed Shandy," he said.

Jenny must have thought about that for a minute. At last she said, "Okay," and then she was gone, flying out the door, shouting long before she ever reached the house.

I was so glad to hear Maury's comment. I had waited long enough for my afternoon bottle.

But still he lingered. I could hear him talking in a soft, crooning voice to someone. I heard Babs' name mentioned, so I supposed it was her.

I called again. I guess Maury heard me that time. He climbed the enclosure, reluctantly and came back to get my bottle from the post.

"Hungry, fella?" he asked as he leaned over the boards to thrust the bottle at me.

He didn't climb in the pen with me, and he didn't reach down and pick me up. He didn't even lean over to stroke my back or scratch my ear. He just lowered the bottle and offered me the nipple.

I took it gratefully. I was so hungry—and had been so bored. It was good to have Maury home. Now, just as soon as I finished the bottle, we would go to the farmyard for our afternoon playtime. I drank thirstily— and hurriedly. I could hardly wait for a good run.

I had not even completely finished the bottle when the door swung open again and an excited Jenny came rushing in, pulling her mother by the hand.

"They're down here. At the far end," she called as she ran. "Seven of them. They're *so* cute."

Maury suddenly pulled the bottle from me. I knew

that there were a few drops left. But he didn't seem to notice. He set the bottle on another post and ran down the barn floor after Jenny and his mother.

"I'll show you the one *I* like best," he called.

"I picked the brown one," responded Jenny quickly. "Can I keep it? Can I, plea-ee-se."

"Now just a minute. Just a minute," the mother was saying. "We already have all the dogs we need. You know Dad plans to sell the puppies to other sheep farmers. We talked about that."

"I know—but just one. Plea-ee-se. Maury has a pet. He has Shandy. I don't have anything," pouted Jenny.

"What about Socks?" asked the mother.

"Socks? Socks doesn't even like to play anymore. She just—just chases mice—an'—an' sleeps in the sun."

"I haven't noticed anything wrong with Socks. You were playing with her just yesterday, if I remember correctly."

"Yeah, but a puppy—."

They reached the far pen. Maury had already rushed ahead of them and now he met his mother with a puppy in his hand. I watched as he held it out to her.

"This is my favorite," he exclaimed.

I didn't see much to recommend the thing. I mean, it was puny—compared to me. It wasn't skipping or jumping, or anything. Just lying there, bobbing its head about a bit.

The mother took it and lifted it up against her cheek. "He is cute," she admitted.

Jenny was in the pen by then. "Look at the others. Look at the others," she was squealing. "Here. Here's the one I like best," and she thrust another squirming little bit of fluff toward her mother.

The mother accepted this one, too.

"Oh," she smiled. "Isn't it cute?"

Each puppy had to be picked up and held and admired. Then they would go over the whole litter again. I was completely forgotten. I hadn't even had my romp—and it was beginning to look like I wasn't going to get one. I called to Maury—but he paid no attention.

"I must get back to the kitchen," the mother said, handing the puppies back to Maury and Jenny. "Here, give them back to their mama."

I heaved an inward sigh. Maybe things would finally get back to normal.

The mother left but Maury and Jenny stayed on. Still, Maury did not come to me.

"We'll have to move them," I heard Maury say. "Dad will be bringing the sheep back in before dark. They will need this pen again. Babs can't stay here."

Jenny agreed. "Where should we put her?" she asked.

"There's room at the other end. Beside Shandy," Maury responded.

Well, at least he still remembered that I existed!

"You take three and I'll take four," Maury was telling Jenny, and they began to scoop up puppies.

"Wait—," cried Jenny.

"What's the matter?"

"I can't get over the fence with the puppies in my hands."

"Guess I can't either," admitted Maury. "We'll put them all down. Then I'll climb over and you hand them to me—one at a time. Then we'll pick them up on the other side."

"Do you think Babs will come—or will we need to carry her, too?" asked Jenny.

"She'll come. Once she sees that all of her puppies

are being moved."

So the next several minutes were spent moving and settling puppies. Jenny even came and stole my blanket.

"This will make a nice soft bed," she told Maury, "an' Shandy doesn't use it much anymore."

I wanted to argue about that. I did still use the blanket—not all of the time—but I liked to cuddle on it when I felt lonesome—or cold. It was comfortable—and homey.

But Jenny didn't seem to hear my protests. She just shook out my blanket, then plumped it up and nestled it into the straw. They began to deposit all seven of the puppies snugly into the blanketed nest.

Babs had followed her moving offspring. She didn't even say thank you for the blanket. Just curled right up on it beside her wriggling, whimpering young and began to lick them, one right after the other.

"Boy," I said to myself, remembering faintly how I had been pushed away because there were three of us, "How will she ever handle that whole wiggling nest full?"

But Babs didn't push any away. She nuzzled them even closer against her. Soon they squirmed into position and I heard them sucking noisily.

Jenny giggled. "Aren't they cute?" she said again.

I was getting mighty tired of the word. I thought it was a word that belonged to me—and now to hear it said over and over concerning the puppies, made me very upset.

Maury was stroking Babs' head. She seemed to like the feeling. She looked up at him with soft eyes and whined—way down deep in her throat.

"Maybe she's hungry," exclaimed Jenny. "I bet she hasn't eaten much today."

"Bet she is," agreed Maury. "We'd better get her something."

"You get it. It's your turn. I got Mom," said Jenny.

Maury didn't argue. He stood up, reached for my bottle—with the bit of milk still in it—and brushed his pants, then headed out the door. Jenny just stayed where she was, fussing over those puppies.

Maury was soon back with a dish of food and a pan of water.

They had been right. Babs rose to her feet, gently scattering mewing puppies who hadn't yet finished their dinner, and began to lap up the water with a thirsty tongue. Then she ate most of the food, drank again and nosed over her little brood so she could lie down. Unlike me, the puppies were able to return to the meal that had been interrupted. I envied them on that score.

"We'd better let them rest now," I heard Maury say and I heaved a big sigh. Finally—finally I was going to get some attention.

But it didn't work that way. They got up from the puppies, brushed the straw off their jeans, then headed directly for the door.

"I can hardly wait to show Daddy," Jenny was saying as they closed the door carefully behind them.

I looked across at Babs. She looked smug. The squirming puppies were still busy pushing and pulling away at her. I guess they wanted to be sure that they got the last few drops. Babs didn't seem to mind. She reached out a long tongue and licked them all again.

The whole thing made me angry. What was so special about these—these little scraps of fur that they could—could just go and upset the whole world? They sure didn't look like much to me.

Chapter Eight

Jealousy

I finally lay back down—on the straw. I no longer had my soft blanket. Babs did. Babs and her nest of constant squealers. They were never quiet. One or the other was always whimpering or complaining about something. I wanted to ask Babs to please hush them up so that I could get some rest—but I didn't. She seemed much too busy to pay attention to me—and besides, I just didn't feel like talking to her.

I had been cheated out of my full bottle—though I honestly had to admit that I didn't really feel hungry. I had lost my own—my very own—blanket. I had missed out on my playtime. And I had received very little of the attention that I had become used to receiving. It wasn't fair. It wasn't at all fair. And just because—just because of silly, new puppies.

I sulked as I curled up in the corner, as far away from the noisy nest as I could get. I tucked my head up against my body and closed my eyes, hoping to shut out the sound. I could still hear the soft mewing sound. It certainly wasn't what one would call a bark. It sounded more like complaining kittens than sheep dogs.

Then suddenly the noise stopped. I strained—listening for it to start again but the tired puppies finally went to sleep. Only occasionally was there a tiny, soft whimper.

I breathed a big sigh of relief and snuggled up tighter. Now I could finally catch a nap.

But it didn't work. I couldn't sleep. I guess I was just too upset by the whole affair. At last I got up and began to munch at the hay that was still in my feeder.

It didn't taste good. I thought of the green grass that I nibbled each afternoon as I enjoyed the farmyard with Maury. Compared to the grass, the hay tasted old and stale and dusty. I turned from it and lay down again.

That didn't work either. Soon I was back up, pacing back and forth in my pen, calling for Maury and reminding him that I still needed my exercise for the day.

"Sh-h," said Babs. "Sh-h. They're sleeping."

"So let them sleep," I fired back angrily. "It's about time, I'd say. They've been crying and complaining ever since they arrived."

Babs said nothing in reply. She just nosed her puppies gently, snuggling them tightly up against her. I could see the pride in her eyes.

When she did speak, she surprised me. "You have a right to be angry," she said quietly. "I know you missed your exercise time."

I just stood there—speechless—not knowing what to say next.

"Well I—I—," I stammered to a stop.

"Puppies always get a lot of attention," Babs said matter-of-factly. "It's always that way."

I guess I could have forgiven Babs, if she hadn't said the words as though she thought it was only as it should rightfully be.

"Well, I don't really see why," I responded. "Look at them. They can scarcely move. Just squirm about. They can't talk. They aren't any bigger than a—than a—."

I couldn't think of anything to compare the puppies to. They weren't even as big as Jenny's Socks.

"Size has nothing to do with it," replied Babs, unruffled.

"Then what does?" I challenged. "I can't imagine them being able to herd sheep."

"Not yet," said Babs evenly as she licked another puppy. "Not yet. But they will. Look at them. You can already see that they'll learn quickly. Look at the shape of those heads. The nose. The—."

But I interrupted. "Pshaw," I exclaimed. "They don't look that bright to me."

I suppose we might have gone right on arguing but just then the barn door flew open. Maury and Jenny were back. I turned from Babs and went to meet them, thankful that they had finally remembered me.

Their father was with them, almost being dragged into the barn while Maury and Jenny both talked excitedly at the same time.

"—and it has white markings on its little front paws and a dark spot right here," Jenny was saying.

"I'll show you the one I like," Maury cut in.

The puppies—again!

I looked over at Babs. She was smiling softly to herself, but she stole one little glance at me. I ignored her and went into the far corner to lie down.

Over the noise of Maury and Jenny I heard the father's voice.

"Well, look at that. Seven. Good job, Babs, old girl. Good job."

They stirred up the whole nest of puppies again, handling one right after the other. Soon they were all whimpering and whining. I wished that they had left them alone.

"She was down in the last sheep pen," Maury was saying. "We moved her here."

"Well, this looks like a good place for her," assured the father.

"Do you think that we should take her back to the doghouse?" Jenny asked.

"Well—no. Buster shares the doghouse. Babs might prefer to be alone for awhile."

"We'll take care of her here," Maury was quick to say.

"Boy—will you," I wanted to put in. "Fuss, fuss, fuss."

I knew that I would have preferred to have Babs and her precious puppies moved back to the doghouse where they belonged. I didn't say so. I didn't suppose they would listen to me anyway.

"She'll need lots to drink," said the father, "and an extra ration of her food."

"And me—I didn't even get my daily grass," I grumbled to myself.

"We'll take good care of her," Jenny promised.

"I'm sure you will," said the father and I silently agreed.

The father placed his hand on Jenny's head and ruffled her hair. Then he stood to his feet.

"I guess it's time for Buster and I to get the sheep back in their pens," he stated. "It will soon be dark."

Was it really that late already? Maury never waited until dark to take me out for my run and grass. We'd hardly have any time together at all.

They all left the barn and I heard the whistle that summoned Buster. Soon the barn was full of commotion and bleating sheep as the flock was ushered in.

What a chattering there was. All of them wanted to talk at once. The ewes were telling one another about the grass they had found, how sweet and succulent it was. A number complained, saying they wanted to stay out—even with the night coming on. Their coats were warm enough to stand the night air, they said. Others argued, saying that it would feel good to be back in a warm bed; the night was already feeling chilled. Back and forth—back and forth the conversations flew until I was sure that Buster must wish that they would all just hush up and get back to where they belonged.

He didn't seem impatient though. He took his time. Slowly and deliberately working each little cluster of sheep toward their particular pen. I couldn't help but admire him as I watched him direct them, hold back, then press them gently forward again.

At last they were all in. But they still didn't stop their chatter. They fussed about and tramped restlessly, pushing against the boards of their holding pens, seemingly longing for night to quickly pass and morning to come again.

The lambs behaved more sensibly. They chased after their restless mothers until they were able to get their supper and then they separated themselves into corners and curled up in the straw. I could only imagine what a busy and exciting day it had been for all of them.

Out of all the commotion, there was one bright spot. Not one of the clamoring ewes had cast an eye at the proud Babs and her nest of noisy off-spring. If they had even seen her, they had not let on. The thought brought me some measure of satisfaction. At least everyone didn't think that puppies were what made the world go round.

I smiled to myself as I curled up in the straw. I'd just catch a nap while I waited for my last bottle of the day. It was nice to have the milling, bleating sheep to cover the sounds of the whining puppies. I hadn't slept much during the day. I was really quite tired and now that things seemed a bit more normal, I could finally get some sleep.

When I was brought my last bottle for the day, the whole family came to the barn. Jenny and her mother and father played with and fussed over the puppies while Maury, very hurriedly, gave me my bottle. I wasn't picked up or petted—but the puppies were. All of them—by turn. And Babs was fed and watered and talked to and stroked until I was sick with envy.

At last they all left the barn again and darkness closed us in for the night. Even the sheep in the pens quieted down, though there was still an occasional reference to the meadow grass and exactly where they intended to graze the next day. Now and then, a lamb decided that he needed a bit more to eat and called for his mother. She quickly answered and the two got together. Then things would become quiet again.

The puppies didn't seem to know day from night. I could still hear them squirming and nursing by turn. Babs just licked and nuzzled, speaking words of love and comfort. I tried to shut out all of the sounds and get to sleep. Once I heard Buster bark and I sensed that Babs lifted her head and listened carefully. Then she lowered it on the straw again, seemingly satisfied that there was no threat to her precious babies. I curled up as tightly as I could and hoped that morning would soon come.

It was several days before things really returned to

normal again. The puppies continued to get a good deal of time and attention. I longed for things to be as they had once been—with me in the spotlight, getting lots of petting and pampering from Maury.

Chapter Nine

Back To Normal

The change was slow in coming. For several days I thought that it would never come at all. But, eventually, things did return to normal.

At first it was only short romps with Maury. I think they might have been simply because his mother reminded him that I needed some grass and exercise. He left the puppies almost reluctantly and took me out for runs.

But gradually the playtime extended and we spent more and more time running about the big farmyard. And then a most wonderful thing happened. Maury called it Summer Vacation. He didn't leave for school each morning.

It was wonderful. Not only was Maury around more—but with the puppies taking less of his time, I was able to spend more and more time with him.

Maury had other chores—but I was allowed to leave the pen in the sheep barn and follow him freely about the farm. Wherever he went, I was right behind him. Oh, true, I made a few side trips, just to check out this or that, but I always kept Maury in sight. I didn't want

to get too daring on my own.

The world had changed. The once bare-looking trees in the yard were now covered with greenery. The yard around the house, with its white picket fence that shut me out, was abloom with color where the white piles had been. Maury called them "Mom's flowers" and often warned me that I was to stay out of there.

I was curious about the flowers—but Maury didn't let me into the yard to investigate them.

Babs' puppies grew quickly. It wasn't long until they were up on their feet running about and rolling in the straw. They were still pretty clumsy though. It seemed to me that they were down as much as they were up. But they didn't seem to mind. They just tumbled and rolled and nipped one another and batted with their clumsy front feet. Babs still seemed to think that they were just about perfect, and the whole family seemed to like them a lot, too.

Even Buster looked at them curiously now and then, but he quickly retired if they tried to pull on his ear or nip at his paws.

Another thing had changed, too. Besides Babs and her young, I was the only one in the whole big barn now. The others had been given their way and left out in the pasture over night. It was quiet in the barn. Even the puppies didn't whine continually. They slept and played by turn—sometimes noisy—sometimes very quiet. I even watched them in the evenings or early mornings sometimes, enjoying the rough and tumble, although I sure didn't let Babs know.

But it was the days that I looked forward to. The days when I would be taken from the barn and allowed to run with Maury.

I wasn't carried much anymore. I guess I was getting too big for that. At least that was what Maury said.

Other people said it too. "Boy, look at that lamb. You can almost see him grow." It made me feel proud somehow.

"Won't be long until he can be put out with the sheep," the father said one day, and I looked around, feeling pride and a bit of arrogance.

"Not—not for a while—yet. He's still pretty little," said Maury. I was about to argue with him. I was getting pretty big.

But the look in Maury's eyes brought me back quickly to my senses. Would that mean that Maury wouldn't go too? Would I be expected to spend the day out with the sheep all by myself? Somehow I feared that it might. I quickly changed my mind and stopped trying to walk quite as tall.

So I was given more time—more time to run after Maury—more time to grow just a bit bigger—more time to think of Maury as my mother—of myself as a human rather than a sheep.

Maury wasn't always doing farm chores. Each day he had some free time which to me soon was understood as fun time. We went for walks or laid in the sun or played games of tag or spent time in the tree house. It was fun. I think that Maury enjoyed it just as much as I did.

One day Maury took the basket of fresh eggs to the kitchen for his mother and then came back, cookies in hand. "C'mon Shandy," he called to me. "Mom says I can go now."

"Baa-a," I answered and ran after him. He stopped long enough to share a nibble of cookie. It really wasn't as good as fresh grass but I knew that Maury expected me to eat a bit and act duly impressed. I munched, letting some of the crumbs dribble to the ground.

Then Maury was off on the run and I was close

behind him, kicking my heels and jumping, just from the sheer excitement of being alive.

We ran all the way across the pasture where the sheep fed. Feeding ewes lifted their heads, sniffed at the air and moved nervously to search for their lambs, calling them to stay close by just in case there might be trouble. The lambs answered obediently but when Maury and I passed by without threat to any of the flock, the ewes soon returned to their meadow grass and the lambs went right on playing.

Eventually we came to some water. It wasn't peaceful and still like I expected water to be. Indeed, it wasn't even in a trough or pail. It bubbled and danced and skipped its way along like a lamb at play. I think it was even singing to itself. I could hear the murmur but I couldn't understand the words.

"This is the creek," Maury informed me. I thought that a very strange name.

"Dad says that there's a robin's nest here somewhere. Three baby robins."

"Oh, no!" I responded dejectedly. "Not more babies!" It seemed that I had just gotten Maury back to myself again.

"It's gotta be in one of these bushes," continued Maury. "Guess we'll just have to look."

It didn't take Maury long to find the robin's nest. Guess the chirping birds sort of gave themselves away. I just knew that I was in for trouble.

But Maury didn't respond to the robins as he had responded to the puppies. Oh, he seemed pleased enough to see them alright, but he didn't even hold them. In fact, he didn't go right up to their nest. Just stood back and watched them squawking and chirping as they lifted funny little heads skyward, calling for their mother and father to hurry with their dinner.

Maury chuckled a bit at the sight and then he left the robins.

"We can't disturb them," he confided and moved on. I sure wished that he had felt that sensible about the puppies.

We went down to the edge of the creek. Maury flopped down on the ground and began to peel off part of his skin. He threw it carelessly on the creek bank and began to carefully roll up another strip of skin on each leg. I watched him, looking down at my own curly legs to wonder if I should do the same. I was quite sure that it wouldn't work. Maury was special. He could do all manner of strange and marvelous things.

"Wanna wade?" he asked. "Sometimes there's little fish in here."

I didn't know what fish were. From the excitement in Maury's voice, I supposed that they were something good.

Maury went right out into the water. I tried one step but I didn't like it. It was wet—and it was rather cold, too. It moved so quickly, bubbling over the small stones with a motion that made me dizzy. I stepped back. This was one place that I didn't plan to follow Maury.

I decided to nibble at the grass that grew thickly all along the creek bank while Maury had his wade. He didn't object. He did call to me every now and then so I knew that I hadn't been forgotten.

"See that fish," he called once, excitedly, but I didn't see it so I didn't respond. "And there's another one," he yelled again.

At last Maury seemed to get tired of chasing the little fish he was exclaiming over and came back to the shore. "Boy," he said, flopping down on the bank and rubbing his feet, "the water's cold."

Then he proceeded to pull his skin back on again. He stood to his feet and rolled the other skin back down over his legs and then straightened up.

"Wanna go see the cattails?" he asked me. "They're in the marsh just down the creek a ways."

I had no idea what would make one want to take a special trip just to see some cat tails. Nor was I able to figure out what had happened to the rest of the cat, but I trusted Maury. If he thought they were worth seeing, then I was willing to follow.

"We'll have to cross the creek," he told me and I hesitated mid-stride. I wasn't sure that I wanted to cross the creek. It was cold, and I didn't like the fast-moving water.

"C'mon," called Maury, leading the way along the bank. "We can cross down here without taking shoes off. There are some stepping stones."

I didn't know what stepping stones were either but if they kept one from putting his feet in the cold water, or being washed away by the whirling stream, I was all for them. I followed Maury down the creek.

The stepping stones were nothing but a few protruding rocks. They lifted their smooth, round heads up from the gurgling of the creek waters and Maury ran right up to them and extended a foot.

They didn't look safe to me. What if they shifted suddenly? What if they sunk? What if one got dizzy looking down at the whirling water and missed the stone? "Not me," I decided. "I'm not risking my life out on that thing."

"C'mon," called Maury. He was already half-way across.

But I shook my head. "Baa-a," I called after him.

"C'mon," he called again. "It's easy. See! Just jump from stone to stone."

But I wasn't convinced.

I wished that there was some other way to get to the opposite side. I wanted to follow Maury. I didn't want to be left behind—alone. But the swirling water and the uncertain stones—. I just couldn't trust them. "Baa-a," I called again.

Maury came back. "Don't be scared," he told me. "The stones are safe. Besides, the water's not deep. C'mon."

But I wouldn't go.

Maury must have been quite set on seeing the cat's tails. He tried and tried to coax me unto the rocks, but each time I just shook my head and backed up another step.

At last Maury scooped me up in his arms.

"Guess I'll have to carry you across," he said, and began the trip across the water, stone by stone. The whole thing made me so dizzy I shut my eyes. I tried to tell Maury to be careful. I tried to reason with him that cat tails couldn't be that interesting to see. I tried to assure him that I'd wait for him by the creek, but he kept right on, bounding from stone to stone.

"Hold still," he told me. "You're wiggling," and he jumped to another smooth rock.

Somehow we reached the other shore. I breathed a deep sigh of relief when Maury deposited me back on solid ground.

"Boy, are you getting heavy," he puffed and then we were off again as he led the way to the cat tails.

I was disappointed in the cat's tails. They didn't even belong to cats. They looked like some kind of growing thing to me. They were on tall stalks of funny grass and they were fuzzy and brown and they were all attached so they couldn't go anywhere or do anything.

"Mom always likes cattails," Maury said and he sat

down and whipped his skin off again and went wading. He passed slowly from stem to stem, breaking off selected cattails as he went, until he had a nice handful. Then he returned and laid them aside as he replaced his skin to its proper spot. While he was busy with this, I checked out the cat's tails. They even smelled like some kind of growing thing. I decided that they would not taste very good. I tried one just to be sure. I was right. It didn't. And it felt very fuzzy and funny in my mouth. I spit it out again.

Maury finished with his skin and gathered up his find. "Mom will love these," he said.

I wondered why. They tasted pretty awful to me, but I didn't say so to Maury. I didn't want to spoil his fun.

All was fine until we came to the stepping stones again. I had forgotten about them but when they loomed up before us I felt panic going all through me.

Chapter Ten

The Fright

Maury looked first at me and then down at his handful of cattails, then at the stepping stones before us.

"This is going to be a bit tougher," he mumbled. I wasn't sure if he was talking to me or himself.

"C'mere Shandy," and he held out a hand to me.

I looked at the stepping stones. Then I looked at the swirling water. Even the thought of the crossing made me feel dizzy. I shook my head and backed up a few steps.

"Then you'll just have to cross on your own," Maury informed me and he started out across the rocks, leaping easily from one to the other.

I watched him, waiting until he was safe on the other side.

"C'mon," he called. "C'mon Shandy. It's easy."

"Easy for you, maybe," I argued inwardly, but I didn't move an inch. I just stood there stubbornly, crying for Maury.

At last he gave in, just as I hoped he would.

"Oh, alright. C'mon. I'll carry you again."

I didn't care much for that idea either. I knew how frightened I had been the last crossing.

Maury crossed back over the stones and reached out his hands for me. In one hand he still held the cattails.

"Why didn't I leave these on the other side?" he asked himself rather crossly. I wondered the same thing.

"Oh, well," Maury went on and shrugged his slim shoulders.

"C'mere Shandy. C'mere," he coaxed, but I just backed away, crying.

"Don't be afraid. We made it before. We can do it again. Now c'mon. I need to get home. Mom will be expecting me to get busy weeding the garden."

I didn't know about the garden, but I sure did hate the thought of that crossing.

"Baa-aa," I said and backed up another step.

I was cornered now. I had backed my way right into a clump of willows. Maury reached down and scooped me up in his arms before I could make a run for it.

"Now hold still," he scolded. "You keep jumpin' and squirmin' and I might drop you."

The very thought had me terrified.

It had been easy for Maury to jump across the stones before. It had been easy when he wasn't holding a handful of cattails and a heavy lamb. Now he took each stone carefully, peering around me to see where to place his foot next.

Below us the water swirled and bubbled. I could even hear it giggling. I think that it was taking great pleasure in the fact that I was so scared.

We were about mid-stream when I couldn't stand it one more step. I had been watching Maury's feet—just to make sure that they would land on the rocks like they were supposed to, when suddenly one forward step seemed about to miss. Maury righted himself instantly, shoving his foot quickly forward to catch the top of the waiting rock, but it was too close for me. With a lunge and a bleat I struggled to free myself and I did, although it wasn't at all what I had in mind.

For a moment Maury teetered, one foot suspended in the air, his arms tightening around my wriggling form. Then the next minute he was slipping—slipping—his foot waving in the air, trying vainly to find some secure place to rest. And then it all happened so quickly that I couldn't keep track of what happened first. I was aware of falling. I heard Maury yell. I saw cattails flying through the air around me. I heard a giant splash. Then cold, swirling water was all around me, even over my face. Maury's hands let go and I struggled upright, bleating and crying in sheer panic.

To my surprise, when I came to my feet, my shoulders and head were above water. I didn't pause long to think about that, though. I was sure that I was going to drown. I was sure that Maury would be swept downstream also. In my panic I didn't even know which shoreline to head for. I turned and fled as though my life depended on it, as I was sure that it did. I didn't stop until I felt firm ground under my feet. The creek waters were laughing gleefully.

Once I had plunged to safety on the shore I turned to look for Maury. He still sat there, right in the middle of the stream, gloomily watching his cattails as they bobbed on downstream.

"Aw-w," he cried. "The cattails. Rats! Now Mom won't—." But Maury stopped and looked down at himself. It was the first that he seemed to realize where he was sitting.

He stood up then and began to scan the shore. "Shandy," he called. "Shandy, where'd you go?"

I answered from behind him. It was then I realized that I had dashed for the wrong shore. That miserable stream still lay between me and home. I cried again.

Maury changed directions and walked back across the stream to me. He didn't bother with the stepping stones. Just waded right through the water. As he came, he shook himself, and water sprayed around him.

"Boy, am I soaked," he said, looking down at his sodden clothes. "Mom's not gonna be too happy about this."

He reached the shore and stopped there, studying the damage. His portable skins were running with little rivulets of water. His feet went squish, squish as he took each step. Then he looked at me. I was still trembling. The water was running off my skin, too. My curly coat seemed twice as heavy as normal. I shook and shivered, still not sure if I was alive or dead.

Suddenly Maury began to laugh. I usually liked to hear him laugh. But not now. Not over this. I couldn't see one thing funny about our situation.

"Boy, do you look funny," Maury pointed out. I could have told him that he looked pretty funny himself. His skin stuck tightly against him, the water running everywhere, but I was more mannerly than to do that.

"We both look pretty funny," Maury continued, looking down at himself, and he laughed even harder.

"Well, wet or not, I got weedin' to do," he said at last, and before I could duck he grabbed me again.

"No-o," I bleated. "No-o, please. Just leave me on this side. I'll stay right here until you finish the weeding."

But Maury didn't listen. He held me tightly and started back toward the stream.

"No sense usin' the stepping stones," he reasoned, "we are both all wet already," and Maury headed straight back across the creek. I shut my eyes. I couldn't stand it. But I didn't lunge. I didn't even wiggle. There was no way that I wanted to end up in the water again. The next time I would drown for sure.

I didn't open my eyes until I could feel Maury climbing slowly up the bank. The water was no longer gurgling around his legs. We were back again on solid ground. We were even on the right side of the stream.

Maury put me down and knelt beside me. I was still leaving little streams of water wherever I stood. I didn't like the feeling of being wet. Maury reached out and began to squeeze the water from my wool. It didn't make me feel any drier but my coat began to feel lighter as he squeezed out handful after handful.

"Boy, are you wet," he commented. "You soak it up just like a sponge."

I didn't know what a sponge was—but if it soaked up water, I didn't want to be one.

"That's as good as I can do," Maury finally decided. "You'll just have to wait for the sun to do the rest."

Then Maury started off on a lope, and I was forced to run to keep up.

We left a little trail of water in the dust of the path. It got less and less the farther we went. Finally it seemed to disappear altogether.

By the time we reached the farmyard we were both beginning to dry out some but I still hadn't stopped my shaking. It was the worst experience I had ever had in my entire life. I hoped with all of my heart that Maury would never suggest the creek again.

When we got to the house, Maury had to go in to change his skin again. I couldn't change mine so I just stayed outside and shivered.

The sun was warm and it did help to dry me off and thaw me out. By the time Maury appeared, I was almost comfortable again.

"Well, Mom wasn't too upset," Maury informed me. I guess he thought I should be glad about that.

"Let's go do some weeding," Maury continued and led the way around the house and toward the fenced-in garden.

We passed Jenny. She was sitting in the garden swing, a puppy in her lap. She still spent a lot of time with the puppies.

"Where ya goin'?" she called.

"To weed," answered Maury. "Wanna come?" He was teasing. Both Jenny and I knew that.

"No way," she responded quickly, and I understood that Jenny wasn't anxious to get involved with weeding.

Then she called again, "I'm playing with Patches."

Maury stopped then and swung back to Jenny. "Patches? Who said he's Patches?"

Jenny's chin went out. "I did" she said defiantly.

"It's no use namin' him," Maury was quick to tell her.

"I can name them if I want to," she argued.

"Them? You mean you've got them all named?" Jenny just nodded her head.

"That's silly, you know," Maury reminded her. "They'll all be named again by whoever buys them."

"I don't care," insisted Jenny, "I can still name them. And maybe they'll like my names and keep them."

Maury thought about that for a minute.

"So—what did you name them?" he asked.

Jenny brightened then. Maury was interested.

She took a deep breath. "Patches an' Prince an' Pal

an' Buffy an' Curly an' Topsy an' Tiny," she recited triumphantly.

Maury thought over the names for just an instant, then he spun on his heel.

"They're dumb names," he called back. "Nobody'd wanna keep 'em."

I stood long enough to see Jenny's lip come out again and then I turned to follow Maury.

I didn't know what was involved in weeding a garden but I was about to find out. Maury opened the gate that had always shut me out and I followed him. My, such long, long, luscious-looking rows of—of something.

Chapter Eleven

The Garden

"The carrots," Maury was mumbling. "Mom said to do the carrots."

He moved from one row to another and then stood still.

"Boy," he said and he didn't sound happy. "Look at all the carrots!"

He stood shaking his head and then dropped down on his knees and began to pick at something. As he pulled it, he cast it to the side and went on to something else.

"That doesn't look so tough," I reasoned. "I'll bet I could do that."

I fell in behind him and reached down to yank up the—the carrots.

But once I got some in my teeth I could taste the sweetness of the growth.

"Now why do they want to throw those away?" I wondered. "They taste real good."

Maury was too busy to realize that he was getting help from me. On and on down the row he went, pulling and throwing, pulling and throwing. Suddenly

he stopped and looked around. I stopped too.

He sat there on his heels for a minute, wiping the moisture from his brow.

"I should'a brought a cap," he muttered. "The sun's hot."

The sun was hot. It felt good. I was finally drying out.

Maury stood up.

"Jenny," he called loudly. "Jenny."

The answer finally came. "What?"

"Would you bring me my cap?"

There was silence.

"Jenny?"

She answered him then, but I don't think it was what Maury wanted to hear. "You weren't nice to me," she said and I could hear the pout in her tone.

Maury thought about it for a minute.

"I'm sorry," he said at last.

"But you didn't like my names," Jenny pressed further.

"I don't care about your names," Maury insisted. "You can call them anything you want." There was a pause. Then Maury continued. "Get my cap—please."

There was no further answer from Jenny. Maury gave up and went back to his weeding.

To our surprise, Jenny appeared a few minutes later. She still had the puppy cuddled in her arms. She also had Maury's cap. Maury reached for it, anxious to place it on his warm head, but Jenny pulled it back, tucking it in behind her.

She tipped her head to one side. "Say you like my names," she insisted.

Maury hesitated. He seemed to be thinking hard. At last he began to speak.

"I think—I think that the names you picked are—

are—. That you've done a good job of picking."

That was good enough for Jenny. She extended the cap. Maury took it quickly and placed it on his head. "—for a girl," I heard him mumble, but Jenny was already on her way back to the garden swing.

"Thanks, Jen," Maury called after her, and then added as an afterthought, "Don't you think it's time that pup went back to Babs for something to eat?"

Jenny turned and looked at him, then she agreed reluctantly. "I'll take him back and get another one," she said evenly.

Maury continued weeding. I went right on helping him. There wasn't room to work beside him, so I followed along after, picking what Maury missed. I thought that we made rather a good team although I was doing a larger share of the work. It seemed that Maury missed quite a few.

I didn't really mind. I just pulled and munched my way down the row. I didn't mind weeding carrots.

We were almost at the end of the row when Maury straightened and looked around. He was still grumbling about the carrots as he stretched his back. He looked around the garden. I guess he was looking for me.

"Shandy," he called. "Shandy, where are you?"

I answered from right behind him.

He turned to look back at me and I felt a good deal of pride. Now he would see the fine job I had been doing. He did. He sprang to his feet and looked down the row. I hadn't missed many. There were just a few short bits of green still showing.

"Shandy!" exclaimed Maury. For some reason he didn't sound happy—just—just excited. I looked back at the row. Hadn't I done a good enough job? Surely he wasn't upset because I didn't throw down the greenery like he had done.

"Shandy! he said again. "What have you been doing?"

I thought it was quite apparent. I had been weeding the carrots—just as Maury had been.

"Shandy—you've been eating the carrots," he exclaimed.

"So-o," I questioned.

"Mom will kill ya," he went on. "You'd better get outta here quick."

But it was already too late. We both heard his mother coming at just that moment.

"Oh, boy!" groaned Maury.

"How're you doing?" Maury's mother called as she entered the garden.

"I—I thought I was doin' fine," said Maury, "until I turned around."

"What do you mean? Are you missing weeds?" She still wasn't close enough to see for herself.

"He sure was," I wanted to tell her, "but I caught most of them."

I was still chewing on the last mouthful.

"It's Shandy," admitted Maury. "I wasn't paying attention to him and when I turned around I found that he'd been following down the row. After I pulled the weeds—he pulled the carrots."

Maury sounded sad and defeated. His shoulders drooped as he faced his mother.

She was close enough to see the row for herself. She stood silently, studying the damage. "He sure did—didn't he?" she said at last.

"I'm sorry," mumbled Maury. "I just didn't—didn't think that he'd eat things."

"Lambs don't belong in gardens," his mother reminded him. "When you do your weeding, you'd better leave Shandy in his pen."

Maury shuffled from one foot to another. I knew that he didn't like being separated from me anymore than I liked being without him.

"It's good it's the carrots," said his mother. "He has just nipped them off. Most of them should come back again."

Maury seemed a bit relieved.

"Now, you'd better get him out of here before he has a chance to do more damage."

"C'mon Shandy," Maury called and started from the garden. I followed him as he knew I would.

"You'll have to stay in your pen for the rest of the day," Maury told me. "You can't be eatin' up all of our carrots."

I was taken back to the sheep barn and put in my pen. It seemed to be getting smaller and smaller. I was beginning to hate it.

I didn't care much for the company either. Babs was still there. Her puppies were running all over the barn now. They even crawled under the boards into my pen.

It's not that they caused me any harm. It's just that they were an annoyance. And Babs just looked on with pride.

Jenny was there too. She was busy playing with the puppies. I heard her calling them all by name again. "Here Patches. Here Pal. No don't chew my shoe, Tiny. Here Curly. Stop that, Buffy," and so on. I didn't want to listen. They seemed to be having so much fun. And here I was stuck in the silly old pen while Maury was weeding carrots. It didn't seem fair somehow. Not fair at all.

Every day I was allowed to follow Maury as he gathered the eggs and fed the chickens. I could be with

him while he washed the car or filled the trough with water for the pigs. I could run along after him when he let the cows in for milking, but whenever he went back to do another row in the garden I was shut up in my pen again.

I didn't like being in the pen. I don't think Maury liked me there either.

"I'll soon be finished with the weeding, Shandy," he'd tell me, "an' then we'll be able to be together again."

We were still allowed our time of play each day. I guess Maury's mother thought that Maury needed it as much as I did. After Maury had put in some time in the garden, I would hear his mother's call and I knew that Maury was free again to spend some time with me.

I got so I listened for her voice, knowing that with the call came my freedom.

The weeding was finally finished and Maury had more time to play again. I was glad to have our playtime back and I guess Maury was, too.

I was with Maury almost from sunup to sundown now. It was great. I tagged along while he cared for the chickens. I watched as he fed the big gray rabbit. I followed while he changed the straw in my pen. Wherever Maury went, I went too.

One day Maury's mother came to the front gate. "Maury," she called.

Maury and I stopped our playing and ran over to see what she wanted.

"Have you seen the big buff hen, lately?" she asked him.

Maury thought for a moment and then shook his head.

"I wonder if she's stolen away her nest?" said the mother.

"It's late for nesting, isn't it?" Maury asked. "All of the other chicks hatched long ago."

"Well, sometimes hens do strange things," said Maury's mother. "I hope a coyote or hawk hasn't gotten her."

Maury looked worried.

"Would you look around and see if you can spot her?"

"Sure Mom," agreed Maury, and off we went.

It was the most fun game of hide and seek I'd ever played. We ran all around the farmyard, looking under this, peering around that. Jumping over this, crawling under that. We even went into buildings that I had never been in before.

Maury opened one small building and peered inside. I jumped up on the step beside him.

"Hey, stay out of there," he cautioned. "This is the old coal shed. Do you know what a white lamb would look like if he went in there?"

I didn't. But I felt a real curiosity about the place.

Maury pushed me back before I could even get a good look and closed the door.

"Let's find that old hen," he challenged and we ran on again.

We eventually found her at the end of the garden under some large rhubarb leaves. She had stolen away her nest all right. From under her wings peeked small yellow heads. Maury was quite excited.

"Mom. Mom," he called as he ran toward the house. "I found her. I found her. She's in the garden. You were right. She's got babies."

Even Jenny came running. Everyone seemed excited about the new chicks.

When they all went to see the hen and count how

many chicks she had under her wings, I was stopped at the gate.

"You'd better stay out Shandy," said the mother. "You know how you love the garden."

She closed the gate with me on the wrong side. I stood there and called for Maury. But he didn't come. I was left on my own again.

I cried again. "Baa-a. Baa-a," but no one came. I turned and wandered aimlessly into the farmyard. It was so sad to be shut out. I hated to be left behind.

And then I thought of that funny little building—the one that Maury had called the coal shed and I decided to do a little investigating on my own.

Chapter Twelve

The Black Sheep

It was just as I had feared. Maury had closed the door behind us. He was always closing doors. I didn't know why he always had to be so careful.

I butted my head against the door, banging it this way and that. Occasionally I had seen a pig or one of the ewes worry a door open if it hadn't been fastened tightly.

But I could make no headway on the door. It was fastened securely. I finally gave up and lay down in the shade. I needed time to rest and think.

Soon a new thought came to me. Maybe there was another door. I jumped to my feet and proceeded to do some checking.

Around the side of the building I came to a little wire fence. It was blocking my passage. I butted against it, determined not to let it stop me. It was solid. Too solid. I decided to try the other side.

I ran around the front of the building to the other side. The small wire fence stopped me there, too.

I was about to lie down again when I thought about that fence. Maybe if I followed it along I would find an opening. Perhaps a gate that wasn't closed.

I started down the fenceline, checking here and there until the fence joined another fence at a corner. I still hadn't found a gate.

I wandered back along the fence, dejected and disappointed.

I went around the building again and followed the fence in the other direction until I came to another corner. No gate anywhere. I was about to give up. I followed the fence back to the building again.

And then I came to a strange place in the fence. It wasn't a gate but it was a spot where the wire had been forced up. It looked like something had been passing underneath, stretching the wire more and more. Chickens perhaps, or even some of the turkeys.

It wasn't big enough for a lamb my size but, if the wire had stretched that much, perhaps it would stretch more.

I knelt down on my front knees and poked my head underneath. I had to turn it slightly sideways to fit. Then I put my full weight against the wire and pushed very hard.

At first nothing happened and then I felt a slight give. I pushed and wriggled some more. It stretched just a bit. I pushed even harder.

By now I had managed to wiggle until my body was under the fence. I pushed again—but nothing happened. I pushed harder. Still nothing. I pushed until I had no more strength to push. It just wouldn't stretch any more.

Finally I gave up and decided to back out. I pushed myself backward but could not move. I pushed again, trying hard to squirm myself free. The wires were poking into my back. It was not a good feeling. I lunged foward then shoved back but nothing happened except that the wires dug even deeper.

I was stuck. Stuck fast. My face was almost in the dust of the ground. My knees felt bruised from the

effort of lunging. My back was stinging where the wires were cutting into me. "Baa-a," I began to cry. "Baa-a." I wanted Maury. I wanted him to rescue me from my awful mess.

I don't know how long I might have stayed there, struggling and crying had not Buster noticed my plight. He began to bark and run back and forth between the garden fence and where I lay tangled. At last he got Maury's attention.

"What is it Buster?" I heard him ask. "Is something wrong?"

"You'd better go see," I heard his mother call to him. Before long Maury was at my side, his hand reaching out to still my struggling.

"What in the world are you trying to do, Shandy?" he asked me. "The garden's not on the other side of that fence."

I knew that. It wasn't the garden I was after.

Maury held me so that I wouldn't struggle. "Mom," he yelled. "It's Shandy. He's stuck in the fence. We'll have to cut him out. I can't leave him; he'll hurt himself more. Could you bring the wire cutters, please?"

I was glad that Maury wasn't going to leave me, but I did hope that they hurried. I wasn't happy with my situation. I tried to struggle free again.

"Hurry," called Maury.

His mother was soon there and while Maury held me, she snipped at the wires that held me fast.

They soon rescued me. Oh, it felt good to stand on my feet again. I was trembling from the experience. I felt that my legs might not even hold me.

Maury must have thought so, too. He reached down and lifted me into his arms. It wasn't easy for him to carry me anymore but he headed straight for the barn, his mother and Jenny trailing along behind us.

Maury placed me on the soft straw. "He's scratched his back," he said soberly. "It's bleeding."

"I'll get the ointment," said his mother as she hurried to a small shelf near the door.

Soon she was back and Maury rubbed some of the ointment into the scratches on my back. At first it stung and then it began to feel better.

"What was he doing anyway?" Jenny was asking. Her voice sounded like she was about to cry.

"He was trying to crawl under the fence. I have no idea why," responded Maury.

"Maybe he thought he could get to the garden that way," Jenny reasoned.

Why did everyone think that I wanted to reach the garden? The garden was in the other direction.

"Well, I'll bet he won't try it again," spoke the mother.

I was left in my own pen then to rest and calm down. Later that evening Maury brought his father to the barn and they carefully checked my scratches. "You did the right thing," the father said. "He's not hurt too badly. The ointment should help the healing. He'll be fine in no time."

In three days my back started to feel better again. It was a reminder to me each time I shifted about in the hay. Soon it started to feel fine and Maury let me follow him about the yard again, I soon forgot all about it.

It was almost a week later that Maury left me on my own again. The puppies had been weaned. They were eating now from a dish just like Buster and Babs. I gathered that this was both good news and bad news for, though they were quickly becoming more fun to play with, they were also old enough to be sold. One by one they had been disappearing from the barn as strangers selected one or the other from the litter.

Maury and I were playing tag when another strange car drove into the yard.

"Are you the folks with the collies for sale?" the man asked.

"Collies?" I thought. "All we have here are some awkward pups."

Maury said "yes" and led the way to the barn. That left me alone again.

I was going to lie down in the shade when I remembered the hole in the fence. I decided to take a look at it.

It was still there. At first I felt angry at the wires. The fence had been rather mean to me. I couldn't quite forgive it for pinning me down and unmercifully scratching my back. Then I noticed something strange. The hole was much larger now. In cutting me free, they had widened the opening.

"I'll bet I could fit through there easily, now," I reasoned, and immediately I decided to find out.

Sure enough, with just a squirm and a wiggle I popped right through to the other side.

I regained my feet and went searching for a back door to the small shed.

There was one. It wasn't very big—but it was there. It was fastened but at least it was down on my level. I figured that I might be able to handle this one. I began to worry it with my head, butting it this way and that, pushing against anything that was sticking out.

It took a long time but at last one side of the door began to sag. With just a few more pushes and bunts it came toppling down and there I was with an entrance into the old coal bin.

I entered cautiously. I wasn't sure what coal was and thought it might jump out at me, but nothing in the bin moved. There was only a heap of old black stuff. I couldn't see where there was any threat to that. In fact it looked like it might be fun to climb. I decided to give it a try.

It *was* fun. I ran up one side and down the other. The black stuff flew all around me, whipping evil-smelling stuff into my face. I didn't like the smell—but it was fun. I decided to try it again. Around and around I raced, up one side and down the other, the black coal making a thick dust in the air. I ran back down and surveyed the whole big pile.

There was one steep side that I hadn't tried. I decided to see if I could climb it to the top. Backing up, I got a head start and away I ran. Like a mountain sheep, I plunged up the side and toward the top.

I was almost at the top when something began to happen. I felt myself sliding, sliding and I scrambled to get a foothold but it was no use. The coal slack was falling and I was falling with it. Down we went, sliding toward the floor of the bin. When things finally stopped rolling and the dust settled, I found myself practically buried under the black stuff.

I began to struggle then, but my feet wouldn't move. I was stuck fast in the coal slack.

Panic seized me. How would I ever get out? Would they find me? Where would Maury look when he discovered that I was missing? I tried to move again but nothing would give way. It was then I started to cry, trembling with fright.

Buster heard my bleating. He summoned Maury. Maury came running and quickly began to scoop away at the coal with his hands, scolding me as he did so.

"What in the world are you doing in here? I told you to stay out of this bin. You could have been buried alive, you know that? Aren't you ever gonna learn?"

I had no answer to that. At last Maury dug away enough of the coal that I could struggle free and stand on my own four feet. I stood there shaking and panting.

"Just look at you," said Maury in exasperation. "You are black from top to bottom. What's Mom gonna say now?"

I looked at Maury. Why was he pointing a finger at me? He surely must be about as black as I was.

Chapter Thirteen

The Fleecing

"What in the world happened to you two?" Maury's mother gasped.

"Shandy got into the old coal bin," Maury responded dolefully.

"Obviously!" was her comment.

Maury looked down at both of us. We really were quite a mess.

"Well, put him down—back in his own pen. I don't want that mess scattered all over the farm."

Maury carried me to the pen. I wasn't sure that I wanted the mess in my pen either.

Babs saw us coming and, with a scornful look in my direction, coaxed her remaining pups toward the other end of the barn.

Jenny was playing with the last three puppies until Babs led them away. Her back had been to the door but, when she heard us enter, she turned around. She sucked in her breath with a sharp little gasp. "What happened?" she shrieked.

"Shandy got in the coal bin," Maury explained again.

"But what happened to you?" she demanded.

"I had to get in to get him out."

"Why didn't he just come out by himself?"

"He couldn't. He was stuck," Maury explained.

"Stuck? How could he get stuck?"

Maury had answered enough questions. He let that one pass.

"Boy, will Mom be upset," Jenny said next. "Do you want me to tell her?"

"Mom already knows."

"She does? Was she mad?"

"No-o," said Maury. "At least not very mad. She did say we are a mess."

"I'll say."

Jenny stood studying us as Maury deposited me in the pen. I blinked. I had some coal dust in my eyes and they were stinging.

"What are you going to do now?" Jenny was asking.

"I don't know. I have to ask Mom. She told me to put Shandy in here."

Maury and Jenny left the barn together. Some time later, they returned. "C'mon Shandy," Maury said, "Mom says you are to have a bath."

I had no idea what a bath was but I was relieved to be allowed to leave the barn. I ran forward eagerly when Maury opened the gate of my pen.

We all went toward the house, Maury leading the way and Jenny skipping along beside him. Maury seemed to feel that some kind of explanation was needed.

"Mom had me clean up and put on these old clothes," he told me. "Jenny is going to help me so she has old clothes, too."

I didn't know why they needed old clothing, but it really didn't matter. They both looked just fine.

As we neared the fenced yard I saw a large tub. It was sitting on the ground and was filled with something. I had never seen anything like it before. I left Maury and went to take a sniff.

The white stuff smelled funny. It also tasted funny. It even looked funny. It was all bubbly and foamy and, as soon as I touched it, bits of it disappeared.

Jenny giggled as I sneezed. "That's soap, silly. It's to help get you clean."

I didn't know what she was talking about. How could that funny stuff get me clean?

"C'mere Shandy," said Maury, and he reached right down and picked me up. Then he bent over that tub and began to lower me. It was then I realized that he intended to put me right into the funny stuff.

I protested. I knew nothing about the soap—except that it made me sneeze, but I didn't want to know more. I started to struggle and kick as I bleated out my protest.

"Now Shandy, be good," Maury scolded. "We've got to clean you up. It's your own fault for going in the coal. I told you to stay out." And then Maury leaned over and placed me feet first into the billows of soap.

What a shock I got. Under those soap suds was water. Lots of water. I was terrified of water. I began to buck and kick, struggling to free myself. Maury wasn't ready for such a fight.

"Grab him, Jenny. Grab him," he cried and Jenny lunged forward to grab handfuls of my black wool.

"Baa-a," I cried. "Baa-a," and I leaped forward again.

Soapy water was flying everywhere as I plunged and struggled. The more I jumped the more wet and soapy I got and the more slippery my coat became.

Jenny squealed. "I can't hold him," she hollered.

"He's gettin' away."

I gave another frantic lunge forward and managed to pull myself free of Jenny's hands. With a new burst of energy, I jerked myself free from Maury and then I leaped the side of the tub and plunged to safety.

I knocked Jenny over backward as I sprang from the tub and she shrieked in pain or rage, I wasn't sure which, and I didn't stop to check. "Baa-a," I cried as I headed for the barn. "Baa-a."

I could hear Maury right behind me. He sounded cross. "Shandy, come back here. You have to get cleaned up. Mom will never let me play with you again, if you don't.

That sounded terrible. Still—. I sure didn't want to get anywhere near that tub.

I kept right on running and Maury ran after me. A quick glance showed me that he was almost as wet as I was. But he wasn't leaving the trail of dirty water that I was leaving with each step.

The barn door wasn't open so I couldn't dodge in there. I headed for the chicken coop. I don't know where I expected to hide.

Then Buster joined the chase. He headed me off and before I knew what had happened I was cornered. Maury was closing in quickly and there was no way for me to escape.

He picked me up again and started toward the tub. I was leaving dirty streaks all over his shirt front. Each time I bobbed my head or wiggled my feet another smudge appeared.

Jenny had left the tub but she was soon back. With her came the father.

"—an' I couldn't hold him," she was fussing. "He just jumped an' jumped an' then he got out."

"Okay, Okay," the big man said. "I'll hold him."

Now I knew there would be no escaping. They were going to drown me—right in that tub of soapy water.

Maury lowered me again and the dad held me firmly with strong, man-sized hands. Maury began to scrub at my wool with a long-handled, hard-bristled brush. I was sure that there wouldn't be anything left of me by the time they were finished. On and on he scrubbed, my back, my legs, my tummy, even my head.

"He sure is a mess, alright," agreed the father. "How he got covered from one end to the other, I'll never know."

"He was almost buried in it," said Maury as he scrubbed.

"He's lucky he wasn't buried alive," said the father.

Maury seemed to be thinking about that as he scrubbed.

"I think that's the best you can do," the father finally said and Maury tossed the big brush aside.

"Now we need to rinse him," continued the father and he hoisted me out of the tub and set me on the ground. Maury proceeded to pour clean water over my thoroughly sodden fleece.

I cried louder. I didn't like the feel of the water as it splashed over me anymore than I had liked standing in it.

"That should do," said the father at last. "Here, take him."

Maury grabbed a big, faded towel and wrapped it around me. I could hardly wiggle. The father let go of me and looked down at his clothes.

"Now I guess it's my turn for a bath," he said.

He *was* rather messy. All covered with soap suds and dirty streaks of water.

Maury laughed. "Me, too," he said, "but I have to dry him off first."

It wasn't an easy job drying me off. Maury squeezed all of the water he could out of my heavy coat, but much of it still remained. Jenny came to check on his progress.

"He looks lots better," she said. I should have felt good about that—but I didn't. I stood there shivering with fear and the cold.

"I have to get him dry," said Maury.

"Do you want me to bring Mom's hair dryer?" asked Jenny.

Maury considered it, then he shook his head slowly. "I don't think it would work," he said, "an' besides, I don't know if Mom would want us to use it."

"What will you do then?"

"I'll dry him the best I can and then—we'll let the sun dry the rest I guess," answered Maury.

Jenny nodded solemnly. "It's good that it's a warm day," she said.

It didn't feel very warm to me. I was shivering and shaking even as Maury continued to towel me. I looked up at the sun in the sky. I wished that it would turn up the power.

"That's about as good as I can do," Maury decided, and he tossed the soggy towel aside.

"You'd better get cleaned up," said Jenny. "You look awful."

Maury looked down at his dirty clothes. "It's a good thing I was wearing old stuff," he said.

Maury turned toward the house and Jenny took pity on me. "C'mon Shandy," she called. "I'll run with you to help you dry off."

I didn't feel like running but Jenny was thoughtful to want to help so, when she headed off across the farmyard, I ran along behind just to please her.

It helped to run. Before long I had stopped my

shivering. By the time Maury returned I was enjoying our little game. We played until we were all tired from running and then Maury called to me.

"C'mon Shandy. It's time to go back to your pen. I'll get your bottle."

The idea of warm milk appealed to me. I gladly followed Maury into the barn and allowed him to close the gate on my pen.

I was nearly dry now and my curly fleece was almost clean and white again. I glanced down at myself as Maury left the barn. It was good to look like myself again. I determined to stay away from the coal bin in the future.

Chapter Fourteen

A No-no!

I didn't catch my death of cold as I was sure I would. In fact, I seemed to have no ill effects from the washing at all. But I made absolutely sure that I kept a distance between myself and that coal bin. I had no desire to merit another bath.

The last of the puppies disappeared and Babs took her place beside Buster again. I thought she looked lonely, but I never heard her complain.

Jenny was the one who did the complaining. "I wish I could have kept just one," she whined. "I have nothing to do now."

"Why don't you play with Socks?" her mom asked her.

"Socks," pouted Jenny. "Socks is no fun."

"You used to think that Socks was fun."

"Well, I don't anymore," insisted Jenny.

"Maybe we should sell Socks, too," said the mother calmly.

Jenny said no more but later I noticed her with the kitten, Socks, firmly clasped in her arms.

The days became normal again. Maury and I did the

farm chores, then we spent time playing together. He even coaxed me back down to the creek on a couple of occasions, though he knew better than to try to get me to cross.

Maury still had to spend some time on garden chores. He wasn't weeding anymore. He was helping his mother pick the produce. Jenny helped also. It did cut into our playing time and I often got bored and lonely while I waited for him to finish.

We were having a good game of tag one day when Maury was called to bring in some carrots for dinner. He went to do his mother's bidding, leaving me alone again. Jenny and Socks were on the garden swing, but I couldn't get through the fence to join them.

I guess Socks tired of swinging for I heard Jenny squeal and Socks came bounding across the grass. Jenny was close behind her. Socks leaped the fence in a few swift jumps and Jenny slowed down to open the gate. On they raced, Socks rushing toward the barn with Jenny in hot pursuit.

I enjoyed watching the game and then they disappeared around the corner of the barn. I turned my attention back to the still-swaying swing. Jenny had left so quickly that she hadn't waited for it to stop.

Then I noticed something else. Jenny had left the gate open.

Stealthily I approached it. I couldn't believe my good luck. All summer long I had been curious about the bright scraps of color that Maury called 'Mom's flowers' but I had never been allowed to investigate them. Now the gate was wide open, just beckoning me to enter.

I moved forward warily, sniffing at one colorful clump after the other. There were flowers everywhere. They were awfully pretty to look at. I moved from one to another, sniffing as I went.

I decided to taste them. Surely something that looked that nice, might taste good too. I took a tiny nibble. It did taste good. On I moved, sampling flower after flower. Some were tasty, some I didn't care for. Those I didn't like, I spit out again. Some were handy for nibbling, and some were more difficult to reach. I supposed that the higher ones might be the best tasting of all.

I reached up to sample one that hung above my head.

I could barely reach the plant and when I did, I gave a quick pull. To my great surprise the whole thing came crashing down.

The commotion awakened Buster. The next thing I knew he was barking at my heels. It frightened me half to death. I bounded forward and another pot came crashing down. "Baa-a," I cried in terror as I started across the terrace. Buster was right behind me, barking and telling me that I was trespassing and should get back to the barn where I belonged.

I would have gone, too, only I couldn't remember where the gate was. I just kept running around and around in circles with Buster close behind me. Pots were falling this way and that as we circled round and round.

It was then that Maury's mom appeared.

"What is going on?" I heard her ask and then she took one look at her flowered terrace and gave a shriek.

"Shandy," she yelled, "you get out of here. Out, I say."

She happened to have a broom in her hand and she used it to shoo me toward the open gate. "Out," she cried again. "Out before you totally ruin everything."

And she waved the broom in front of my nose again.

I was afraid that she was going to hit me with it. I ducked my head and scrambled for the open gate. As I ran, I tipped over one last pot of flowers. I saw them too late to avoid them and I heard the crash as I stumbled past.

Maury's mom yelled again but I didn't turn around or even slow down. I ran for the barn as quickly as my legs would take me.

Maury came looking for me later. "You've really done it now," he told me. "Now Mom says that you have to go out to pasture with the other sheep. She says that's where you belong. Says you've caused enough trouble."

He petted me as he talked and I knew that he was sorry about it. I felt sorry, too. I hadn't meant to mess up the potted flowers. It was really Jenny's fault. She had left the gate open.

But Maury continued to talk as he stroked my sides. "I guess it won't make much difference. I have to go back to school again Monday, anyway. It would be too lonesome for you to just wait in your pen all day. You'll be better off with the other sheep. You'll soon get used to it."

I didn't like the news that Maury had to return to school. I remembered how long the days had been without him.

I wondered what was so special about school anyway. Hadn't Maury gone there enough?

I didn't seem to have much to say about it. Maury had already made up his mind. His mother had made up her mind as well. I knew that without asking.

"You can stay in the barn tonight," Maury promised me, "but tomorrow you'll need to go out with the others."

I didn't understand why I should be going with the sheep. Why couldn't I just stay with my own kind? I'd be good. Honest. I would never bother the flowers again.

I went to bed feeling sad and lonely that night. I couldn't sleep for thinking of Maury's words. Then I cheered up just a bit. Maybe by morning the whole thing would have blown over. Maybe Maury's mom would forget about banishing me to the pasture. Maybe Maury would decide that he didn't want to go back to school after all.

I settled down on my bed of straw and tried to get some sleep. There was really no use fretting about things. There was nothing that I could do about it anyway.

I heard Buster bark once and Babs joined in, then all was quiet in the farmyard. I didn't hear another thing until I heard the rooster crow, and I knew that morning had come again.

I stirred myself. I was wondering if Maury might bring me a bottle. He kept informing me that I was getting too big to need the bottle but he always yielded and brought me another one anyway. I would just have to wait and see—and hope.

Chapter Fifteen

Out To Pasture

I had been awake for a couple of hours the next morning when I heard Maury and Jenny talking as they approached the barn.

"—don't go to school until Monday," Jenny was saying, "so why does he need to go to the pasture now?"

"Mom says so," responded Maury. That seemed to settle the matter. But Maury went on. "Sides, if he goes now he has a chance to sorta get used to it while I'm still here."

"Oh-h," said Jenny. She seemed to feel better about the idea. I didn't. I had been hoping that the whole thing would blow over and I'd be given another chance. I'd stay out of the garden and the coal bin and the flowers—if only—.

The door was opening. Maury was the first one in. He came over to my pen and reached a hand down to rub my head. He didn't say anything but his eyes looked sad.

Jenny didn't even chatter. She just looked on, her eyes big with sorrow. Then she asked a silly question.

"Does he have to stay out overnight, too?"

Overnight? Of course not! I had never stayed out overnight in all of my life. It was cold out there. It was dangerous. I had heard the dogs barking. Strange things sometimes came around at night. Of course I wouldn't be staying out overnight.

But Maury was nodding his head. He continued to stroke me, his hand lingering on the spot where the wire fence had scratched me. It was all better now. I didn't even feel it.

"Will he—will he—care?" asked Jenny.

Maury said nothing.

"Won't he get cold?" went on Jenny.

"Look at his coat," said Maury running his fingers through my thick fleece. "He's ready for any kind of weather."

Jenny seemed to feel better about that. But I still wasn't too sure.

There was silence in the barn. Jenny waited, shifting impatiently from one foot to the other. At last she heaved a big sigh. "Well, are ya gonna, or not?"

That seemed to rouse Maury back to the job at hand. He stopped stroking me but left his fingers entwined in the curls on my back.

"Of course," he answered. "Mom said to, didn't she?"

Maury opened the gate and allowed me to pass through. Then he led the way across the farmyard and down the lane toward the sheep pasture. I had followed Maury down this trail many times before but somehow I knew this time was different.

Jenny trailed along behind us, stopping occasionally to study a crawling thing or pick a wild flower.

We reached the meadow and Maury opened a gate. "Go on in Shandy," he said. "Go on."

But I just stood and looked at him. I was a follower. Not a leader. Maury hadn't gone in.

At last Maury seemed to understand. He passed through the gate and stood just inside the pasture fence. "C'mere Shandy," he called but I was already on my way.

Maury went back then and shut the gate behind us. Jenny stood on the other side, the wild flowers dangling haphazardly from one hand. Her eyes were wide with wonder.

Already, sheep were beginning to make their way toward us. They came a few steps at a time, their noses lifted, their eyes alert. Now and then a ewe would call out to a lamb, warning him to stay close by. Then they would proceed forward a few more steps, testing the air, stirring restlessly. I knew that they were nervous about the strangers in their pasture, but their curiosity wouldn't allow them to move to safety at the far end of the enclosure.

"It's okay," Maury called to them softly. "It's okay. It's only Shandy and me."

But the sheep still shifted about, sniffing the air and bleating for their lambs.

"C'mon Shandy. Let's get acquainted," said Maury and he turned and led the way toward the sheep.

I don't know if he moved too quickly or if the sheep feared that he meant them harm, but the whole flock fled in one swift motion. They turned tail and ran, bleating and scrambling as though wolves were after them.

Maury stopped in his tracks. He flung his cap on the ground in disgust and stood watching them flee.

"What ya gonna do now?" called Jenny from the fence.

Maury retrieved his cap and dusted it off against his leg. "Nothin'," he answered. "No use chasin' after them. They'd just run some more."

The sheep hadn't run far. They formed little clusters and milled about, seemingly discussing among themselves what this strange action meant. I could hear the bleating, though I couldn't make out their words.

"Maybe they'll come back," ventured Jenny.

Maury thought about that. He flopped down on the ground, his back to a fence post. "Guess we'll just have to wait," he said and seemed prepared to wait all day if necessary.

It didn't look like much fun to me. I would rather have been playing tag or going to check the chickens. I liked to hear them flutter and squawk when we entered the coop. But Maury seemed set on waiting. Then I remembered how hungry I was. There was plenty of green grass in the pasture. I began to feed.

Jenny waited—and waited. The sheep drew nearer, sniffing and stamping and then a strange thing happened. They seemed to lose all interest in us and went back to their feeding.

"How long are you just gonna sit there?" Jenny asked Maury, impatiently.

I was wondering the same thing.

"As long as it takes," growled Maury.

"Well—I'm goin' back to the house. This is boring." And so saying, Jenny skipped away, scattering some of her wild flowers behind her.

The meadow grass was sweet and delicious. It was even better than the grass around the farmyard. I hurried to get my fill so that Maury and I could return to the buildings. Maury just waited, watching me nibble.

"I've got my other chores, you know," he said at length. "I'm gonna have to do them before Mom calls me."

He still sat there. I quickly grabbed a few more mouthfuls of meadow grass. I wanted to get just as much as I could before I had to go.

"I'll come back to see you later," Maury continued. Strange words.

He stood to his feet and dusted his jeans. "G'bye Shandy," he said.

I looked up from my eating. Maury never said "good bye" when we were out together. Just "c'mon."

Maury was climbing over the fence—not even opening the gate. Just climbing right over the fence. I ran toward him, crying as I ran. I tried to tell him that I couldn't climb fences. He'd have to open the gate for me. There just wasn't room to push myself under the wire.

But Maury kept walking. He didn't even look back. I called and called but he didn't answer. Back and forth, back and forth along the fence I ran, hoping to find some way to get out, but there was none. I kept running and crying, pushing my nose against the fence here, thrusting my shoulder against it there, but nothing would give. I finally stopped crying. Maury had passed from my sight among the farm buildings. I still kept running back and forth, seeking a way of escape.

By the time I stopped I was exhausted. I didn't know whether to rest or eat some more. At last I decided on the eating. I was still hungry. I could rest after I filled my tummy.

I kept pretty much to myself. The sheep ignored me. It seemed they didn't feel threatened as long as I kept my distance.

A couple lambs started over my way. I think they were curious and wanted to ask questions, but their mothers spied them and quickly called them back.

Maury came in the afternoon. The flock was down at the far end of the pasture, lying in the shade of a cluster of trees. They didn't even get to their feet as Maury approached.

I was so glad to see him that I bounded up from where I lay and ran to meet him, crying my glad hello as I ran. I guess he was glad to see me too. We rested on the ground together, Maury stroking my back and talking to me softly. After some time we had a good running game of tag. Then we rested some more.

The sun had swung around to the west when Maury left me. I fussed about it again. But I didn't cry and run the fence as long as I had the last time. I remembered that Maury had eventually returned.

I cast a glance at the sky. It would soon be dark and would be time to be put in my barn pen for the night. Maury would come and get me then.

But the darkness began to crowd in around us and Maury did not come. I stirred restlessly, pressing myself against the wire fence.

The flock of sheep had moved up from the lower end of the pasture. A few fed aimlessly as though more bored than hungry. Others lay scattered or in groups, chewing the cud from their day's feeding.

They talked back and forth occasionally. Just a comment now and then, answered if another felt like answering, left hanging in the air if no one felt like responding.

"Do you think they're gonna leave it here?" I heard one ask. She was looking in my direction.

"I don't know. I hope not. It was eating our grass."

"There's plenty of grass, dear," said a third.

The second one gave her a haughty look. "Not the way it was eating," she sniffed.

There was silence. Then the first one spoke again. "I guess it's harmless enough."

"I just hope it knows enough to keep its proper

place," was the response.

The first one sniffed. "Well, if it doesn't, it will soon learn if it knows what's good for it."

There was a bit of a titter and shifting of bodies. The words sounded like a threat. I shivered slightly even though I wasn't really cold.

The evening had cooled, however. There was a chill in the air. I was glad for my heavy fleece. I looked at the sky again. It was getting very dark. Maury still had not come.

Restlessly I paced the fence. My eyes turned again to the sky. The strangest thing was happening. Overhead bright little lights began to twinkle. Here and there, all over the sky they were scattered. I wanted to ask what they were but there was no one to talk to. Then another very strange-looking thing appeared. Right over the eastern horizon where the sun usually came climbing, came another big ball. This one was orange-yellow in color and as big and round as Jenny's birthday balloon.

I watched it as it climbed higher and higher. As it rose it seemed to shrink a bit.

"What is it?" I wondered. I even asked the question out loud. But there was no one to answer. "Maury would know," I told myself. "I'll ask him when he comes."

But Maury didn't come that night. He didn't come at all until the afternoon of the next day. By then I had eaten my fill and was lying by the fence.

"You should be lying in the shade," Maury worried. "It's hot out here in the sun."

But the shade was down at the other end of the pasture. That was nowhere near the fence that separated me from Maury. Besides, the sheep were all down there in the shade. I knew they preferred that I stay well away from them.

"Hasn't the flock accepted you yet?" Maury asked.

"I don't know about accept," I wanted to tell Maury, "but I don't think they like me." I didn't say it. I was so glad to see Maury that I didn't want to waste time complaining.

We had a good time running and playing together, then cuddled up on the ground and just sat. Then Maury stood and said he had to be going and I was left all alone again.

Chapter Sixteen

A True Sheep At Last

Day after day passed by. Maury came to see me but he didn't spend nearly as much time with me as previously. He was back in school now and still had farm chores to do.

"Are you happy now?" Maury asked me one day as he sat stroking my woolly back.

"Happy?" I didn't know about happy.

"Do they bother you?"

"Bother me? No. They just ignore me, as long as I keep my distance," I thought within myself. "If I dared to get too close, I suppose they might bother me."

"Do you mind sleeping out under the sky?" was Maury's next question.

That one was easier to answer but my thoughts surprised me. I hadn't really stopped to think about it, but I didn't mind. In fact I liked it. I enjoyed watching all of the bright twinkling lights overhead and watching the orange balloon-ball roll upward in the sky. It was lonely, sleeping all by myself, but I did like sleeping under the sky.

I still hadn't figured it all out. I slept under the same

sky; I ate the same pasture grass; I drank from the same pond; but I was strangely different from the other creatures around me. They were pasture persons. I was a farmyard person. I didn't really belong here. I belonged in the farmyard with Maury. With Maury and Jenny and Buster and Babs. With Socks and the mother and father. I definitely didn't belong out in the pasture. I couldn't understand what I was doing out here.

And then one day a strange thing happened. A frightening, terrible thing. It changed my whole life—though it very nearly ended it.

I was feeding off by myself when I heard the sound of rushing bodies and tramping feet. I looked up, a mouthful of meadow grass dripping from my chin. Toward the fence that enclosed our pasture, three large animals came running.

I was curious, but not concerned. I was sure that they would turn aside once they reached the fence. But they didn't. They all cleared the wire with one mighty bound and came directly toward me. I didn't like their trespassing, and I certainly didn't like the looks on their faces.

Then I heard their words and I liked them even less.

"He's all alone," said the first one.

"Let's get him," said the second.

The third one just chuckled, an evil, gleeful chuckle deep down in his throat. It was then I realized that they were talking about me.

The rest of the sheep were nervously watching the action. I could hear them tramping and shuffling and calling for the lambs. I suppose the natural thing for me to do would have been to run as quickly as I could to them. But I had one thought and one thought only. "*Maury.*" I needed Maury more than I had ever needed him before. I needed him urgently. I needed him quickly. With a loud cry I started to run. Not for the stamping flock but toward the gate that led from the pasture to the farm buildings.

I could hear the three dogs behind me. They were fast on my heels and getting closer. "Baa-a," I cried in panic. "Baa-a."

Even before I reached the gate I could see that it was closed. There was no way for me to jump the fence or duck under it. The dogs were almost at my heels. I was cornered.

And then I heard another sound. The sound of other rushing feet and something swished right over my head. There was a terrible din. Such barking and growling and threatening like I had never heard before. With great relief I recognized Babs' voice. But what could one dog do against three?

But Babs was not to be stopped. She rushed the three advancing dogs that had been on my heels, barking out threats and insults. To my amazement all three of the onrushing animals skidded to a stop before her fury.

On she went, not even slowing down. I was sure that she'd be torn to pieces.

Then I heard another welcome sound. Buster was coming. Already he was calling to Babs, assuring her that he was close behind her.

I guess the other three dogs heard Buster too for, in less time than it takes to tell it, they had turned tail and were racing from the pasture with Babs right on their heels. They cleared the fence, their tails tucked in tightly lest Babs would take a nip at one, and didn't even look back as they headed for the woods beyond the pasture.

Babs slid to a stop beside the fence, still calling out

her threats and telling the three what would happen if she ever caught them back in her sheep pasture again. Then she circled back and came panting over to me.

"Are you alright?" she asked me, all out of breath.

I was shaking badly. I couldn't even answer, and then Buster was beside us, his bristles still standing upright on his neck.

He stared off in the direction the three had fled and then turned back to Babs, his hackles slowly settling. "Good work," he told her as he gave her a lick on the side of the face.

Suddenly Maury was running toward me, his father close behind him. Without even waiting to open the gate, Maury hopped the fence with the aid of a post and dropped down beside me. He didn't say anything. He was trembling almost as much as I was.

The father climbed the fence a bit more slowly and stood looking toward the woodlot. "Crazy coyotes," he said. "That's the first I've seen any of them for quite a while."

"We'll have to really watch carefully," Maury said, his arms still around me.

"That's what we have the dogs for," the father replied and he reached down and patted Babs on the head. Buster moved closer to get a share of the petting.

I looked at Babs. I really hadn't thanked her properly. I knew without question that she had saved my life. I wanted to tell her how much I appreciated it. I would have been happy to pay her all sorts of compliments—like how sure I was that any puppies of hers were bound to make great sheep dogs. I just mumbled my thanks instead and lowered my head. I guess Babs understood. She whined softly.

I was aware of the flock. They had moved in closer, a few steps at a time. Nervously they shuffled about, sniffing and tramping and urging their lambs to stay close by.

The others noticed them too.

"They're all scared," said Maury.

"They'll soon settle down," promised the father. He gave Babs one more pat and turned to look at Maury. "Now we'd better get back to digging those potatoes. I don't think we'll see any more of those coyotes today."

Reluctantly Maury released me. He let his hand trail along my curly back and then followed his father through the opened gate. They closed it carefully behind them and headed for the farm buildings, Babs and Buster at their heels.

The flock began to press in closer. I could hear the shuffling, the tramping, the nervousness. As they drew nearer I could hear them talking. They all seemed to talk at once, but I heard one ewe's voice above the others.

"What kind of creature is it, anyway?"

There were all sorts of replies to the question. I couldn't begin to sort them all out. Then one voice rose above the rest.

"It was the bravest thing I ever saw. Did you see it?"

"Right away from the flock. Really quick thinking," responded another.

"I'd never have thought of it myself," a different one was commenting.

"I wonder what kind of creature it is?" the first one asked again.

A big ewe stepped forward. "Why a sheep, dear," she said knowingly. "A sheep."

"A sheep?"

"Of course. A sheep."

"You mean—you mean—like us?" someone asked incredulously.

The big ewe looked down her nose. "Of course," she said again. "He's one of us."

"But—but you said before—," a smaller ewe began to stammer, but she was quickly silenced by the larger one.

"You saw it. You saw for yourself how he ran directly away from the flock. You saw how he diverted the coyotes. How he ran toward the buildings to alert the sheep dogs."

"But—but—," began another ewe who joined the conversation.

The big ewe turned her head slightly and gave the other ewe a cold stare. "And you saw how the sheep dogs came running to his defense," she said with finality. "Have you ever seen the sheep dogs protecting anything but sheep?"

No one dared venture a reply.

"You see," the big one sniffed. "He's a sheep."

The matter seemed to be settled.

The big ewe turned to me. She lifted her head regally and gave me a smile. "I don't think we'll be seeing much of those coyotes again," she said with some authority, "but all the same, it'd be best if you stayed in close to the flock—with the other lambs."

The other lambs? I was a lamb? The truth began to sink in slowly. I was a lamb. A sheep. Just like all of the others. A pasture sheep.

I liked the thought. I smiled to myself. A lamb about my age pressed in close beside me. "I saw what you did," he said in an awed voice. "Weren't you scared? Boy, I woulda been scared to death."

Another crowded close. "*Cool,* man," he whispered in my ear.

All around me they clamored. Giving me elaborate

compliments and asking if I'd be on their team in the games.

I tried to protest, telling them that I'd been frightened half to death—not brave, but they wouldn't listen. They waved it all aside and pronounced me 'modest' and continued to talk about how smart I had been to draw the coyotes away from the flock. And how brave I was to put my own life in jeopardy in order to protect others.

At last I gave up and just shrugged my shoulders and grinned. I moved right into the middle of the flock. It was going to be fun being a sheep.

I looked about me. They were all there, crowding in around me. The ewes. The lambs. And I was one of them. I would never be alone again—not even when Maury was at school. I had friends—and family —lots of them. I was a member of the flock.

With a pleasant smile on my face I followed the cluster of ewes as they moved back to grazing. Right beside the largest one I reached down and nipped off a mouthful of the succulent meadow grass. No one offered one word of complaint. Yes sirree! I was going to really enjoy being a sheep.

Artist Dedication

Illustrations are dedicated to my mother,
Helen Frantz, who loves lambs and me.

A special thanks to Matt, Erin, and Ashley Gonterman
and to Ben and Neva Graber and all their lambs.